Dislocate

By Matt Johnston

To my wife, Rachael.

"And remember, Francis," my mother says, "Dr Attwood just wants to help you."

I, of course, know what she is alluding to, and I understand her reluctance to make direct reference to what was a rather unpleasant incident. There is also absurd comedy in any situation where it is considered necessary to give explicit instructions not to bite anyone. Though, while I appreciate my mother's concern, it does seem a little tactless and unfair to bring that incident up at this juncture. After all, when it happened, I was as surprised as anyone. Even at school, even in the face of the endless beatings and intimidation, I have never deliberately hurt anyone. So, while not without my detracting qualities, I would challenge anybody to say that I am an inherently violent person.

I am also not even sure that I deliberately bit that man, and I certainly have no recollection of having premeditated intent. It was as though it was somehow a suitable and justifiable response to his prodding and probing. A critique, if you will: a poignant piece of social commentary, or physical theatre; an act, which only made sense in that moment.

To say Dr Bennett had in any way initiated the attack would of course be entirely false, and disingenuous. Rather, I would say that the act of biting, and Dr Bennett being bitten, was inevitable. It was as though both our lives had built to that particular moment, a crescendo had been reached; Dr Bennett had offered his flesh as though in sacrifice, and I was powerless to do anything but submit to the surging power of destiny. I could no more 'not bite' Dr Bennett as consciously decide to stop breathing.

It is a good analogy, for when you hold your breath you feel a similar force; from the very moment you take the defining gulp of air, it is there. At first it is just vague and distant, a lingering threat, browbeating you, wagging a finger with displeasure, but otherwise leaving you to your own devices. However, this soon changes: as the air depletes, it grows dominant and, try as you might, this inner bully soon summons an overwhelming force. It is this primitive power that makes you take another breath, forcing you to keep living. I think it was this same force that drove me, compelled me, beyond all conscious desire, to sink my teeth into the doctor's exposed forearm.

There is, of course, no justification for my behaviour other than that of diminished responsibility, and this is a defence I still categorically refuse to evoke. I do think, however, that my mother needs to keep a more favourable sense of perspective. I have long since lost count, but were we to tally them up; the psychologists, psychiatrists, doctors, councillors, therapists, and the host of other quacks, shaman and soothsayers, I am pretty sure they would number into double figures, if not the early twenties. Therefore, I would argue, based on probability, for me to bite one of them is not statistically significant. This regrettable episode should therefore be considered for what it is, an isolated incident, and not necessarily another latent antisocial and destructive personality trait. Had I thought about this theory at the time I would, of course, have found little benefit in raising it. Between my mother's tears and my father's brooding anger and frustration, this would neither be successfully articulated nor sympathetically digested.

I always know when I am about to be introduced to a new clinician, or subjected to a new form of treatment or therapeutic session. There are two tell-tale signs. The first is that my father will be wearing a suit. This in itself is a rare occurrence, and as such it is quickly noted. I am not even sure that I had ever seen him in a suit prior to these family outings. I still recall almost not recognising him on that first, fateful day I was exposed to the medical and psychiatric fraternity. The other sign that raises my suspicions is that my mother will sit with me on the back seat of the car. She invariably tries to hold my hand during the journey, her cracked smile barely able to hold back the swelling tears amassing behind mascaraed eyes.

4

She repeatedly tells me everything is going to be alright. Where she gets these deluded opinions from, I could not begin to tell you.

That is not to suggest duplicity on my parent's part; this is no kidnap. It is because I have a particular blind spot to the discussions that I have with my parents on such matters. Later, as my father opens the door of the car, or as we step into the reception of the latest clinic or hospital, I will remember the laboured conversations. My parents' beleaguered sales pitch, outlining the rationale for yet another attempt to get their only daughter to approximate a normal teenager. Whatever that is.

Part of the problem, part of the problem recalling the discussions at least, is that while I am somewhat sympathetic to their motivation, I am inherently a passive bystander to their efforts. However, all things considered, if the prevailing stereotypes of children are to be believed, it does seem a little unfortunate for them that I am the product of their union. Whether it remains for me to apologise for this, or they to apologise to me, I am not sure.

Though I'll admit that the first session with a new clinician is not that bad. My experience is that I usually get to 'sit this one out' while the doctor and my parents do most of the talking. At this point, I am generally considered in either the future or past tense, but rarely the present. I usually have to answer a few obligatory questions, much like a soldier does when becoming a prisoner of war: name, rank and number, but otherwise it is my father who bears the brunt of the questions. My mother says little, and when she does it is always in hushed tones, as though discussing family secrets, especially when we get onto the issue of the potential benefits and side effects of pharmaceuticals. My father also takes great care to avoid certain words and, during the conversation, he will frequently have to start a sentence two or three times before he can express himself without using any of the ever-expanding list of taboo phrases.

"I, I just want her to be happy."

Invariably, this is how my father sums up his prevailing hope, and the rationale for my treatment. I am still to reach a conclusion as to whether this is the reasonable ambition of a loving parent or the unstable pipe dream of a fantasist. After all, were he to be truthful, he would be unlikely to conclude that he was happy. My mother is not happy and, while I don't know that many people, none of those I have met seem to be particularly happy either. There seems to be a degree of hypocrisy that, despite this observation, it is I who has to keep taking the tablets.

I continue to breathe, simply out of an inability to formulate a valid reason to stop; in, out, in, out, in....in.......in....... I breathe out. It is a subtle process, a process which requires a conscious effort to even realise it is happening. The gasses flow across my larynx, and I imagine my internal organs hard at work, extracting the oxygen, sucking it into the narrow highways of my arteries and disseminating it around my hungry body. I sit with my eyes shut, imagining that my skin is the outer limits of all existence, taking pleasure in my totality. Unfortunately, with the constant assault of the outside world on my senses, the façade - that I am alone - is hard to maintain. Ultimately, I am forced to acknowledge that the world does exist, but as way of a compromise, my mind slides into the more achievable fantasy: that it is I, not the world, which does not.

It is only when a car goes past at speed that the remanence of this construct is broken, and reality imposes itself on my fanciful daydream. With the bridgehead secure, other sensations pour through the breech, reminding me that my shoes pinch and that my inactivity has allowed the cold to penetrate what few layers of clothing I have pulled across my pitiful chest. Reluctantly, I am forced to acknowledge the regrettable truth, grounding me back onto the hard plastic seat of a windswept bus stop. My head turns involuntarily to the offending vehicle, but it is soon lost from view, leaving my eyes to sweep over the insipid panorama in hope of distraction, if not entertainment. They obey my command, but roll around their sockets with little expectation.

Though it has at least stopped raining. The constant drizzle since early this morning has succeeded in stripping away all semblance of warmth, enabling the plumes of my grey breath to hang in stagnant clumps. The wet and the cold climbs from the darkened pavement, soaking through the cracked leather of my shoes and biting into the exposed flesh of my shins and calves. The bus stop does at least shield me from the wind, and viewing the world through the wall of cracked glass, it offers insightful commentary on my disposition.

Francis Kelly eats shit!

The observation is written about a foot above my head, and written backwards when read from my side of the glass. The handwriting offers a looped flourish, it is punctuated and is surprisingly neat. The words are written in cherry pink letters, most likely using lipstick. Past experience tells me that, if it does not continue to rain, it will be over two weeks before the message is sufficiently smudged to become illegible. By this time, some new insight into my tastes or habits will most likely have replaced it.

However, the point is well made, and while crude in its delivery, I struggle to counter the analysis. Francis Kelly does truly eat shit. She has been eating it for as long as she can remember and there is no expectation that, in the coming hours, days, weeks or years, this is likely to change. That is not, however, to say she has acquired a taste for it.

But I have by now only limited sympathy for Francis, predominantly because she swallows only a fraction more shit than everyone else. Her problems lie in the fact that she has the misfortune to be acutely aware of what she is eating. This is in part because she is reminded again and again with timely notes; written across school desks, toilet cubicles and on local public transport. I wonder why Francis does it. I wonder whether, given time, a fuller narrative might be provided, all in different coloured makeup, offering a more complete, more rounded analysis to what is, after all, an alarming yet insufficient statement. Perhaps Francis's condition is linked to the various other snippets of social commentary about her life and preferences? It must be said, if all are to be believed, she does seem to delight in her degradation.

The glass wall shields from the wind, but not the cold, and I force my hands deeper into my pockets, trying to retreat into an almost singular space. Considering my diminutive

8

size there is not far to retreat anyway. Though my condition has 'improved' sufficiently to eat with enough regularity to keep a thin layer of tissue between my skin and bones. Yet even when wearing more layers than I am currently, there is little to hold the warmth at my core and my muscles tense in spasm. I expect I will be ill again in a day or two; a state which, while not actively courted, is welcomed with a general ambivalence.

"Missed the bus again."

The announcement is part acknowledgement, a weary statement of resignation, and part question. This is sufficient to remind me that I am not alone at the bus stop, but it is not enough to initiate conversation. I smile weakly by way of confirmation but offer nothing in the way of elaboration.

The old woman sitting next to me is a regular feature of my Thursday morning truancies. I don't know her name, or her age; in fact, I know little about her at all. But our repeated proximity at this bus stop has engendered some small degree of commonality. To say we have a relationship would be too strong a term, unless accepted in its most literal sense. Yet, though I am no great judge, I guess she could be described as a good person. I appreciate this is a relative term but, despite suspecting my continual failure to catch the earlier bus is deliberate, she does not lecture or criticise. I suspect her sympathetic nature might represent a degree of empathy for the many years ahead of me. Year upon year of shit eating. I was rude when I first met her, an unnecessary overreaction to a harmless enough comment about something I no longer remember. However, she seems not to have held the outburst against me and, while I have yet to offer it, I recognise that I probably owe her an apology.

She is as small as me and equally as fragile. Her skin is like greased paper, crumpled into little ridges, translucent to the point that blue veins and burst blood vessels join the freckles and liver spots in an intricate topography. There is, however, a resilience about her:

the accumulation of her years and experiences projecting a confidence and core strength that I do not possess. I guess this woman has also eaten her fair share of shit in her time. Regrettably, it is more than likely that she is still forcing it down her line-drawn throat. Her loose alabaster flesh is testament that what does not kill you cannot be guaranteed to make you stronger. I guess, after so many years, you just lose your sense of taste. I am not sure whether she knows that Francis Kelly eats shit or not, but I suspect she does. She has, after all, spent enough time at this bus stop to possess an insight into a whole host of Francis Kelly's behaviours. Though, like with my earlier insult, I am grateful that she has chosen to ignore these facts.

She has only arrived at the bus stop after the mob of my classmates have left for classes, herded by routine, pushing their way onto the bus. Her ability to avoid such a spectacle is a luxury of which I am extremely jealous. The old woman avoids the daily scrummage of their departure, while I literally have a front row seat. At such moments my classmates take great pleasure in mocking the only passenger left seated at the stop, hurling insults through the mercifully sealed windows. I dislike this moment intensely. Invariably, there are a dozen or so smirking faces, and though I try to maintain an air of indifference, I get the distinct feeling that I am some exhibition at a zoo. On most days I try to delay my arrival to ensure the bus has gone long before I reach the bus stop. Though this is becoming increasingly difficult due to the increasing scrutiny of my parents. The small house in which I seek to barricade myself from the world is barely one hundred yards from the bus stop.

There is, however, a certain sensation of satisfaction when, as this cattle truck recedes into the distance, their faces are still distinguishable from the rear window. At this brief moment I get the distinct impression that they are envious that I have chosen to be left behind. That, and their obvious confusion, their inability to understand the inherent differences that clearly exist between us. And in these brief moments before the bus

10

disappears from view, I catch a glimpse of some inner torment. Their once grotesque, mocking jeers now seem undermined by some vague sense of self-doubt. They go and watch me stay. I stay, and on occasion do not even bother to monitor their departure.

Past experience has also taught me that the confines of the bus are not a safe environment for me. Forced into the close proximity of my persecutors, it is as though the law of averages dictate that one of them will choose to subject me to some small indignity. Usually, it is one of a small group who initiate the attack, though increasingly I have noticed other confederates are willing to take the initiative in fostering some broader camaraderie.

I am offended by my own weakness, my inability to form any effective strategy to prevent them from targeting me. The majority of the attacks and insults are insignificant, usually just vulgar name calling or, on occasion, rhythmically beaten chants. On the whole it is the other girls who serve as my persecutors. The boys remaining obliviously indifferent, unless their support is actively sought, pressed into active service by the girlfriend of that particular week.

Though it is not the injuries themselves which so enrage me. Rather, it is the satisfaction my attackers take from my humiliation and the collective entertainment my degradation affords them. It is this that causes my throat to swell, adding a hint of colour to my otherwise unhealthy complexion. But I must confess that, even if they ignored me, I would most likely still seek to be alone at the bus stop. Ultimately, the applied association with this screeching gaggle of apes is sufficiently offensive to justify enduring the cold and the wet.

Another car goes past, faster than is necessary, sending a stinging splatter of cold water across my shins. The old woman's muttered curses mirror my own thoughts, and we shuffle our feet to shake the liquid from our shoes. The old woman has a dog, some wire-haired terrier, and this also shakes in disgust. I like this animal; I like its slow, stiff-jointed hobble, its cataract eyes and oblivious nature. The fur is a mixture of grey and white, as though old age has slowly bleached it of colour. The dog has tottered over to where I sit, sniffing at my legs and allowing me to ruffle its head as though performing some form of canine phrenology. The old woman smiles at both me and the dog, cooing like some new mother over the gurgling joy of her infant child. For a moment I fear she is going to make another insipid observation, or provide some strange commentary to our interaction in some childish squeaking voice. Thankfully, her attention is diverted, the moment passes and I push the dog away while she is not looking to avoid the risk of any repeat performance. The dog's name is Dorothy, and through association, I have extended the name to the old woman.

Her husband's name is Derrek, a fact I know due to repeated reference. This is as much to ensure that this fact does not slip entirely from his enfeebled mind, as any conversational necessity. He stands to his wife's left hand side, his attention transfixed by the complexities of the scheduled timetable. I can only guess at what he makes of such a tangle of letters and numbers; I imagine the experience to be similar to decoding some long dead language.

I assume that he is of a similar age to the old woman, but he has retained his weight, left to hang from what, in his youth, must have been a considerable frame. Yet now, as with all old men, the underlying structure has lost its rigidity. When combined with his tentative and uncertain movements, he projects an innate clumsiness and insecurity. While the old lady sits, he always remains standing, his arms tucked by his side, gently pressing his hands together as though cradling some precious object. His fingers twitch, trying to kick-start some long lost understanding.

There is little in the way of meaningful conversation between them. Derrek is continually subjected to the old woman's monologue, her futile efforts to replace the treasured memories which have escaped from his increasingly porous consciousness. I have

12

regrettably eavesdropped on many of these conversations, as she reminds him of holidays, friends and neighbours. At other times she simply articulates a running commentary of her own train of thought, as though, in the absence of his own functioning cognitive process, she allows him to share her own. His contribution is stunted and limited to endless repetition of the same inane questions. Yet he responds to her instruction meekly and without comment, and follows her about with puppyish obedience. His primary function is now to carry the shopping, seemingly demoted below the rank of the arthritic pet in the fractured chain of command. The only difference between Derrek and the dog is the absence of a lead.

I find myself wondering whether she is lonely or sad. I wonder what she sees and thinks about when she looks at this man, while she dresses or bathes him. I wonder whether she sees the young man she fell in love with, or just a cruel reminder of what the disease has taken from both of them. I tend not to think of Derrek in his own right. His existence has now been relegated to that of an annex or extension of his wife, like some semi-functioning, dislocated limb. He is a human anchor to which she ties the decrepit dog, to prevent it limping painfully into the traffic.

To date I have not reached any satisfactory conclusion as to whether to pity Derrek. The man is, as far as I can see, blissfully oblivious, while the old woman is forced to endure this man as I am forced to endure my classmates. I am under no doubts that this was not what she had hoped for on her wedding day, but it must be acknowledged that, were my peers similarly placid and compliant, I would at this moment be sat within the confines of the warm school bus.

I remind myself to obtain some lipstick at some point. I have the strong desire to write on the bus stop glass: Derrek eats shit. But it is OK as long as his wife doesn't remind him.

III

"So how do you feel today, Francis?"

I have noticed that Dr Attwood has a tendency to use my name when I am not giving our weekly sessions my full attention. This is a tell-tale sign that I have once again failed to maintain the consistent and pre-rehearsed façade of a needful and humble patient. I know she suspects something, and I do not doubt that she has noticed the subtle changes in my behaviour since our first session, some six months ago. I fear that she is slowly chipping away at me, like some skilled and patient archaeologist: brushing away layer after layer, revealing things which I have deliberately hidden and wish to remain buried. I now hope for hubris on her part, that whatever of my evolution she has perceived is explained as therapy based improvements. Her confidence in her medical abilities, attributing my metamorphosis to her skilful intervention. Unfortunately there is more than enough work for her to be getting on with. On paper, to those not party to the true nature of Francis Kelly's unique disposition, it does look pretty damaging. The truancies, the late night wanderings, the self-harm, the eating disorders and the insomnia. Not to mention the lack of personal hygiene and the inability to form meaningful relationships; the list just goes on and on and on.

Dr Attwood's office is now thoroughly familiar to me, and it would be an unpleasant enough place to sit even without the constant inquisition and dissection. It is a fairly big space, which Dr Attwood has filled with angular modern furniture. There is a large wooden desk, though our 'interviews' - for this is how our sessions are described - are usually held on plump and cushioned sofas. There is a childish tastelessness to the room's décor, a conscious decision I suspect, to reflect Dr Attwood's junior clientele. Even without the sizable glass wall looking down over the gentrified canal side, it is far too brightly lit. The walls have been painted in vivid colours, vibrant blues and oranges, which remind me of being in some child's playroom. Apparently, people are supposed to relax here.

That is not to say the room is totally void of things of interest. The view from the office is impressive, with all the major architectural landmarks of my town on show, set against the backdrop of low purple hills. The people in the street below are like insects and cannot be considered independently. Yet, from this elevated position, they become a disharmonious collective, a swarming mass which does, at times, prick my curiosity. The view is so good, in fact, that the blinds remain drawn throughout our sessions; this is to help prevent my attention from wandering.

There is also a sizable fish tank, with numerous strata of variously-coloured fish. They maintain their own layered hierarchy, drifting back and forth above illuminous, sapphire-coloured stones. The fish, I like. My attention is usually drawn to one in particular: a big slug-like creature that stays glued, limpet-like, to the glass. Whether it moves much between my various appointments I cannot tell you, but during each appointment, I guess it has moved at best a few millimetres, and never when I have been looking at it. The other fish float back and forth, drifting in what little current wafts up through the ventilation system. All the while this ugly fat fish just hangs on. It is an obvious metaphor, I know; one which I am careful to hide from Dr Attwood out of fear she will seek to incorporate it into my therapy.

Dr Attwood wears casual clothes, presumably having no reason to impress her patients. Today's jumper is a rich crimson colour. I have no idea what such attire says about someone, other than the potential that they are colour blind. Dr Attwood smiles and nods a lot, and she keeps reminding me that I can call her Linda. She is an ample and healthy woman whose spacious and desirably located office hints at significantly greater wealth than her modest attire. She smells of soap, a delicate cool scent in an otherwise sterile environment.

And it is this sanitised void which seems more in keeping with the doctor's true nature. She is precise and professionally distant, at no point ever risking any situation which might draw her own feelings or opinions into proceedings. She is my second mother, but one with no tactile longing for her injured child.

I, for my part, do my best to limit any source of comment or observation from my appearance. Thankfully, the majority of our sessions are after school, so I usually arrive in her office clad in the armour of my school uniform. She has on more than one occasion stated that I might be more relaxed in my own clothes, but this just goes to illustrate exactly how little she really knows about me. For some reason she seems to be actively trying to promote some sense of identity, blissfully ignorant of just how self-defeating such efforts would be. I never wear makeup or jewellery so, as far as I can tell, this only leaves my hair and nails for comment. Neither are worthy of compliment.

Dr Attwood is speaking, probably in the process of rephrasing or elaborating on her previous question. In moments such as these she leans forward in the hope of creating a false atmosphere of intimacy; her posture is open and welcoming. I find myself in need of a moment to formulate my response so as to avoid whatever trap she is setting for me; I draw a long slow breath and tense my diaphragm. The figure of Dr Attwood stagnates and crystallises, her speech slurs, becomes drawn; stretched into a low painful drone which then finally, as though dropping below the audible spectrum, stops. A smooth and seamless transition into total dislocation.

Now I can rise and stretch my legs. In front of me the doctor continues to gesture to the empty chair. Her unblinking eyes do not track my laboured movements around the room, her warm, non-judgemental gaze loses context and degenerates into the transfixed stare of the clinically unwell. Her mouth hangs rigidly open and empty, her right hand in mid gesture, her left holding the pen which has yet to write anything other than my name and the date on the small notepad balanced on her knee. In these suspended moments the soft textures of fabrics, upholstery, and hair take on a new, brittle solidity. The brightly-coloured fish hang inert in their tank, stone-like pockets of gas remain transfixed like amorphous gems suspended in translucent glue. I compose myself, return to my seat, and align myself into my previous position. I allow my breath to escape with a slow, methodical composure and the doctor finishes her sentence. I make her wait for my reply.

"I feel," pausing as though in genuine deliberation, "better, thank you."

Through our sessions, I have learnt that it is safer to use the terms 'better' or 'worse' than 'good' or 'bad'. The absence of an absolute gives me scope to speak in vague, relative concepts rather than subjecting myself to the painful experience of trying to articulate to Dr Attwood what 'good' or 'bad' actually entails. The same can equally be said for the terms 'better' and 'worse', but for some reason Dr Attwood seems to struggle with these phrases. All of this is important because Dr Attwood is very good at utilising kinks in my armour, and from these seemingly innocuous questions she emotionally undresses me. Ironically, were I more confident I could resist such exposures and I might be inclined to be more honest with the doctor. I would say that I feel the same as the first day I sat in this office and the same as I have every time since. All that has changed is my understanding, my acceptance, and my control of my dislocation.

I might save Dr Attwood a great deal of time by offering her my own diagnosis of my condition, if it can be called such a thing. However, not seeking to undermine the doctor's authority, I am beginning to believe that a more accurate description would be to say that what I suffer from is a total lack of any recognisable condition. My motives, decisions, and movements seem, at best, casual acquaintances rather than purposeful consequences. My relationship with this indifferent and inconsequential universe is at best tentative, as though I am some sort of unanticipated by-product or pollutant.

17

If I looked to clarify this definition, I'd say I would use the term 'relationship' only in order to articulate a distinction between what is, and what is not, 'me'. And, whatever could be articulated as 'a relationship', is at best dubious and questionable. This encompasses not only my obvious human relationships, but also the relative physical relationships I have with my surroundings, which would seek to keep me tethered to a mutually assumed concept of human existence. Yet I find myself resigned to a core belief that I am terminally severed, entombed by some infinitely fine and invisible membrane which somehow has shrink-wrapped my organism. Somehow I feel as though I am held separate in a metaphysical vacuum - that is, in some fundamental way, totally distinct from that which I observe and I am immersed. I extend this to the very objects around me and the fundamental laws of physics. My mass, volume, and position in space seem somehow a charade, an illusion of perverse misdirection. For example, picking up a small stone: I can touch it, feel its smooth contours, and detect its desire to reconnect with the ground from which I have lifted it. I can stand, sensing the connection and dynamics between the stone and my hand, my hand and the stone, but at my core I remain convinced that this subjective position is neither absolute nor relevant.

Yet my lack of 'a condition' is an abstract concept and I cannot claim a total rejection of the physical state of existence. I am acutely aware of the 'physical me', something that can be seen and touched. I recognise and accept those vibrating atoms which have combined to make me an observable part of my ill-defined whole. But while we might stand toe to toe, cast in each other's shadow, I would refute your beliefs that there is commonality between us. We are comparable only in terms of the marks and measures devised by man, to enable them to devise some form of contrast. I remain convinced that, in some indeterminable regard, one of us, or maybe both of us, may simply not be there.

Anyway, we are getting ahead of ourselves. Perhaps I should explain, but, well, it's complicated. I have been in Dr Attwood's office, or an office like it, so many times that I no longer have a great recollection of 'the what' and 'the when'. I am asked the same questions and as far as I can tell I give the same answers. The dialogue is so formulaic and circular that I am beginning to think that this may actually be part of my therapy; the sessions slowly being distilled into some prolonged and repetitive mantra. They are now so predictable that it is becoming disconcerting. The sensation of the experience is now far beyond déjà vu. It is almost like I am literally reliving the same conversation; the only thing that noticeably changes is Dr Attwood's jumper and the weather. The coloured fish are too numerous to enable me to detect any change. This is another reason I watch the slug-like fish, hoping to distinguish between sessions by the minute deviations in its position.

Though, at other times, I recognise that there is a disorder to my thoughts. I get confused and I am easily distracted. My memory is also a curious thing, remembering with crystal clarity and subtle detail distant and irrelevant occurrences, while at times I am unable to retain the most basic recollection of things which were said and done only a few hours before. Because of this, I realise I would make a terrible witness. Were the police to need to rely on me to catch some dangerous criminal, it would be disastrous. I am sure that, even were the crime committed right in front of me, whatever fractious and cryptic narrative I might offer the authorities would surely lead their investigation in the entirely wrong direction. If the case ever got to court, my testimony would be of more use to the defence than the prosecution.

But now I have led you this far on my merry dance, I am afraid you will just have to be patient. I, for my part, will also try to be sympathetic. We both have to simply accept that there is, for me at least, all the time in the world.

IV

Sitting crouched in the toilet cubicle does little to suppress the violent shivering. It rained again before I got through the school gates, only a light squall but this was still more than enough to penetrate through my flimsy coat and blazer, saturating the inner layers. The damp fabric now rubs against my skin when I move, leaving me feeling clammy and uncomfortable. I am definitely coming down with something. My stomach turns with a vague nausea and the headache that had previously roamed freely around my skull has now camped itself behind my left eyeball. It pulses with a belligerent malice. My legs feel numb: an aching sensation that contains no warmth, a product of my cramped position perched on the lip of the toilet seat.

In the end, I did not wait for the next bus and chose to walk the two miles rather than spend money on the fare. That is not to say I got to school any quicker; my motivation was primarily the desire to generate some warmth in my limbs and to escape the ever-present risk of the old woman's conversation. There was something about that lingering wait with the old couple which was beginning to affect me. I caught the woman eyeing a bruise on my wrist. I watched her chew over her thoughts and I decided it best to excuse myself before she launched into a tirade of well-meaning questions. I fear she possesses the disagreeable trait of genuine concern, and the prospect that she might seek to come to Francis's aid was more exhausting than the walk. Eventually, long before I reached my destination, the bus overtook me. Regrettably, I looked up at an inopportune moment, catching a fleeting glimpse of her sad, withered face through the glass as she went past. Her concern was so obvious that I genuinely feared that I might find her waiting for me at the next bus stop.

Time passes slowly in the toilet, but this is a process with which I am now fully familiar, as mine is a patience borne out of a general, passive indifference. It will be another twenty minutes until the break in lessons, a point at which the shrill ringing of bells will announce the clamour of footstep and slamming of doors as the herds shift morosely between indistinguishable rooms. It will be at this point that I will reluctantly join my classmates, ignoring the numerous cheap comments my reappearance will generate.

The girls' bathroom is in the basement and the empty chair in which I should be diligently studying is, fittingly, almost directly above my head. Luckily, the thick concrete ceiling is sufficiently thick to cocoon me from any suggestion of the subject I am missing out on. Not that I am under any illusion that my absence has not already been noticed. None of my teachers are unfamiliar with my modus operandi and I have noted that recognition of my attendance is an almost subconscious reflex of the majority of my unfortunate mentors. Instances of punctuality are greeted with incredulous surprise, as though my presence is some form of unexpected blessing or an exotic luxury. Thankfully, few of them now seek to draw attention to my presence. The previous dry witticisms, while not without their own merit, were just another small contribution in cementing the irrefutable difference between myself and the rest of the class. I suspect they recognised the disruptive effect on the otherwise ill-defined assortment of teenagers under their tutelage.

I, of course, have no idea how my repeated absences are greeted by either the class or my teachers. I imagine the empty chair is alluded to, if not pointed out by my classmates, and I suspect in some classes my absence may have even become something of a communal observation. Though I recognise that this may also be vanity on my part and would not be surprised to discover that my latest absence is greeted with little more than weary acceptance, if anything at all. The trouble is, my absences are so frequent that I am no longer even entirely sure which class it is I am currently missing.

Part of the trouble is that being at school is always much more bearable when it is emptied of pupils and staff. Even though I must traverse this space with stealth I find these draughty corridors achieve a serene and peaceful quiet, in the starkest contrast to the frenzied turmoil between lessons. The building itself is vastly superior when it allows you to explore its nooks and crannies undisturbed by human proximity and the ever present threat of an education. Only in such instances is there a genuine opportunity to study and consider the architecture. That is not to say it is an aesthetic or beautiful building, but it does retain a certain integral quality of its function.

Teachers and other administrative staff lurk in stairwells and behind corners but despite the imminent threat of exposure I rarely dislocate at such moments. To do so seems to be almost cheating, to deny myself the sport of slipping silently through this formulaic warren, or the subtle pleasure of these brief moments of tranquil exploration.

It is a sprawling labyrinth of structural banality, its wide corridors and clumsily sloping ramps reminding me of some of the other great institutions I am forced to frequent. It is as though all of them were built to some ugly, multipurpose template, providing a commonality for those wretched inhabitants who will never truly escape its domineering effect, training them for the next instalment, be it a factory, hospital or prison. At its peripheries, efforts have been made to create a veneer of some fresh environment and the new regenerating constructions are like a fresh coat of paint over warped and rotting wood. But the school, at its core, remains an immovable mass of concrete and asbestos. At its heart, this institution will always remain standing on those suffocating and dogmatic foundations. The fragments of those countless previous generations, processed and shrink-wrapped for adulthood, bleed through the walls to gather in the dust filled corners of empty spaces. Old buildings have memories; every child contaminated by such an exposure is destined to leave something of themselves behind. I wonder what I will leave behind, what my own personal contribution to this legacy will be. I wonder whether what I leave behind will be as incompatible with the school as my presence. I also wonder whether any of me will ever truly escape.

The girls' room used to be better suited to my prevailing mood but they have recently refurbished it. The old worn brick work is now masked with white porcine tiles, the heavy doors and rusted locks replaced with light and clean plastic fittings. It now has the appearance of a mixture between a fast food restaurant and hospital theatre. It smells of chemicals, harsh citrus scented detergents which add to my headaches. Though not yet warm enough to stop me shivering, I notice the swirling drafts have gone. Doors do not slam and the wind no longer whistles at me through hairline cracks in window frames. It is also considerably lighter. The thick wire-meshed glass and small lattice frames have been replaced with a great expanse of frosted glass moulded in clinical and cold aluminium. Because of this, even on a wet day such as today, the dull shadows struggle to create the oppressive and gloomy atmosphere I had previously enjoyed. There are now long strip halogen lamps and tall mirrors, neither of which I appreciate. The former creating a crisp yet clinical glare which hurts my eyes, the latter making it difficult for me to avoid my wholly unsatisfactory reflection. The creaking pipework remains, at least, and despite this new glossy exterior the familiar clunking and clicking noises of its labouring heating system still provides the suitable groan of day-to-day existence.

And the radiators are good, increasingly so now that the vast majority of the warmth does not immediately leach away through the ill-fitting doors and paper thin windows. By the time of my next lesson I might almost be dry. My clothes are only slightly damp from my body heat while my shoes and socks, sat upon the long radiator, will offer some welcome comfort to my frozen and bruised feet.

The bathroom is also now cleaned diligently, a new found enthusiasm for order and cleanliness which I assume is due to the school's not inconsiderable investment. Not that the bathrooms were previously unhygienic, it was just that the monochromatic crumbling walls were never going to portray anything other than a concrete bunker. The new doors have served as a blank canvas for budding artists, and a platform for the latest offering of social commentary. And I guess I could take a certain degree of pride that my shuffling existence continues to generate significant interest and endeavour. Within two weeks of the refurbishment, the cubicle to my left was adorned with libellous proclamations of Francis Kelly's personal preferences. Yet it is the comment on the door in front of me, an elaboration on the bus station's earlier statement, which now holds my attention. I will not lower the tone to repeat what it declares that Francis Kelly has been up to. The spelling is poor but the accompanying diagram, though amateurish, leaves little opportunity for misunderstanding.

Part of me considers adding something to the narrative, something autobiographical to supplement the contributions of my numerous ghost writers. I had hoped to at least write something insightful, to provide a different perspective to what I fear is an increasingly one-sided and distorted account. Yet as the tip of the pencil hovers an inch from the surface my mind goes blank and I struggle to think of anything which will either inform, inspire, or amuse. For a brief moment I consider writing that 'Francis Kelly dislocates' but the ambition is fleeting and without appetite. What's more the pencil is blunt and is unable to leave much imprint on the otherwise smooth expanse of wall. This in itself is a suitable metaphor.

I always lurk here, every time I miss the first class of the morning. I always choose the same cubicle and it surprises me that, in all the time I have hidden myself from lessons, nobody has ever seemed to seek me here. The toilet is hardly the most inventive of locations in which to hide and I do not even bother to conceal myself behind the door, leaving it open so I can stretch out my damp legs and wriggle my toes. There are other girls' rooms in the school, ones yet to be subjected to such lavish refurbishment, but none are suitable for my clandestine lingering. Yet for lunch and mid-morning break periods they are more suitable

24

places of refuge from the swarming gaggling masses of my would-be persecutors. Maintaining a low profile is a full time occupation.

It will now be another ten minutes until the bell, but for want of anything else to do I begin the laboured groundwork for my rehabilitation into the school's schedule. First, I patter across the cold tiled floor to the radiator, retrieving my shoes and socks. My feet are so cold they seem unresponsive, though the radiator has done a good job softening the leather so that I am hopeful I will get to lunch before I am forced to take them off again. I am precise in my routine. Being small, I can contort so that much of my body can be lowered under the hand dryer; the warm blasts of air doing much to drive the chill from my bones. The hand dryer is also mercifully quiet and it is barely audible from the corridor.

Finally, after washing my hands and face, I stare accusingly at my reflection with cold determination. Francis Kelly stares back at me, though I feel her refusal to break my eye contact reflects her belligerence than any great sense of confidence. From studying her at length I guess I can say there is some commonality between us, though despite all this time I have still to form anything close to a meaningful description of this girl. The best I can offer you is a list of features, and leave it to you to formulate your own conclusion. I fear I am no longer objective and Francis Kelly gets enough bad press as it is without adding to it.

For starters, I cannot actually see the entirety of her profile. Her hair, best described as a lank mop, is constantly pulled down over her face. It forms a smoke-like mist of raven hair, the only trace of colour being the hint of the natural brown roots and eyebrows. There are flecks of green in small, tired looking eyes. It is difficult to say whether it is the whitewash hue of her skin or the fragility of her features which reminds me of fine china, but Francis is like some intricate doll: even the blemishes of colourless acne and bloodless lips reaffirm the sense of delicate emptiness. That is not to say that I am under any illusions that hidden under this mask there might be some rare beauty. I have seen beauty, and I have observed the response which it evokes from those in its proximity. I can categorically confirm that Francis Kelly incites no such sentiment.

The rest of Francis is equally unremarkable. It is also undesirable. She is small but not in a petite or slender way. It is as though she is little more than a scrawny and emaciated frame over which the idea of a young woman has been casually thrown. For Francis the embers of blossoming womanhood have seemingly stuttered and died; her figure is punctuated by sharp corners of ill-fitting limbs and joints rather than soft curves or elastic muscles. Therefore her tailoring, based on the generic template which predicts the form of girls her age, renders her uniform ill-fitting. It is as though the fabric itself is somehow reluctant to be hung from her.

That is not to say I am bitter or disappointed when I see Francis Kelly in the mirror. I guess, humiliating and ultimately self-defeating as it might be, were I burdened with the insecurities and vanities of my peers, I too could throw my efforts into endless self-promotion and adornment. This, however, would not only be a significant waste of time but also considerably counterproductive. My efforts, if they can be described as such, do not seek to make any statement. I have no desire to reinforce some vague idea of me or to impose myself on the world. On the contrary, the idea of me being vague and nondescript is wholly desirable. I seek camouflage, invisibility and, ideally, nonexistence.

Sadly, little I have discovered helps cater for my unique tastes. Disappointingly, no publication aimed at girls my age offers any great insight as to how I can improve and perfect my techniques at anonymity. As such, my successes to date have been predominately a mixture of trial and error - and without any real scientific evidence base. As a result I have little confidence that any one strategy is capable of making me more unobservable to the world than any other.

It seems true that certain societal groups are more oblivious to me than others. Boys my own age, for example, seem to possess a recurring blind spot to me, a trait which I find particularly attractive. But for the majority of the human populace I fear I lack a certain mask of normality, failing to fit with any recognisable template of a girl my age. Perhaps this is it, the basic irony that the absence of the endless effort to beautify and promote myself leaves me dangerously exposed. But I am unsure how you foster a command of averages, and I remain nervous that any deviation from the dull, ill-defined form I have cultivated would be construed as an alarming display of a personality or opinion.

At each waking moment it is though I am working my way through an endless series of shifting shadows, constantly assessing and reassessing the various options open to me. On the most basic level my diminutive size is a benefit, enabling me to become lost within the jostling and frenzied enthusiasm of my peers. I have learnt to move slowly, avoiding eye contact and without comment. I have learnt to ape collective responses, offering approximations of emotions and mimicking acceptable behaviours. But my strategies are still far from fool proof and at any given moment I do regrettably pop into existence. It is at such moments that I concentrate my thinking, trying to understand what it is that has ultimately betrayed me.

One thing I have learnt is that you cannot be seen to cower, to spend your days creeping and scuttling in some advance state of fight or flight. I have learnt that girls my own age are natural pack predators, able to detect weakness and insecurity as a shark might sense a drop of blood in an ocean of water. But I am unsure whether it is my weakness which enrages them or whether it is merely a suitable distraction from their own insecurity that continually funnels their ill-defined rage and fury in my direction. I used to think it was the latter but to simply throw the blame at the feet of my persecutors seems to absolve me of some degree of responsibility. It is I, after all, who is the common denominator in these beatings and as such must conclude that, if not initiating the abuse, I am at least a contributing factor.

It is for this reason that I spend more time examining my school uniform than the skin-covered object within it. It would not be an over-exaggeration to say that this is my favourite outfit, and I would wear it on evenings and weekends were it not for the fact that this would be entirely self-defeating. Within school, however, the dark green jacket and tartan skirt is as good a camouflage as I could hope for.

I am not the only one targeted for such behaviour and I wonder whether, in some way, a perverse hierarchy may have formed with me as the unlucky incumbent at its pinnacle. I wonder whether, by action or inaction, it might be possible to be replaced, to slowly move down, through lower dregs of the pecking order into the safety of the faceless swollen ranks. Perhaps were I to achieve my aim of making myself entirely unobservable, my unfortunate mantle might be passed with a symbolic tirade of abuse and fists onto some heir apparent.

V

There is a solid thwack against the window and the glass visibly vibrates. It also makes me jump, causing me to tense, forcing me to the cusp of a dislocation. All eyes turn to the dirty circular smudge, but by the time Monsieur Grimshaw waddles to the window the perpetrators have successfully hidden themselves in the sea of milling teenagers. I watch him stand there, imagining the view of the mingling hive, his hand on the window latch. He is contemplating chastising the boys, scanning the crowd for an offending football, searching for a poorly timed glance onto which he can train his fury. I watch as he chews the words over, his eyes darting back and forth before finally conceding defeat. It is a smart decision on his part, his bellowed orders would be ill-advised and undirected. After a few moments he wisely retreats from the window, disguising his impotence from the braying mob. I suspect the lunchtime detention is held on the first floor to minimise such interruptions: up here, at least the incarcerated are hidden from the mocking rebukes and the distractions of the rest of the school.

Usually the bureaucracy is quicker, but today something has been mislaid. As a result, I received no instruction to report for my penance for the latest failure to get to school on time. Yet I turn up for detention anyway, my willing submission only achieving a quizzical raising of Monsieur Grimshaw's hedge-like eyebrow. He mumbles an approximation of a greeting and vaguely waves in the direction of the rank of battered desks before turning back to the limp sandwich and the magazine open on his desk.

A lunchtime detention is the standard punishment for each of my tardy arrivals. My repeated crimes have enabled me to obtain considerable insight into the administration and division of labour amongst the teaching staff. Over time, numerous teachers have served as my lunchtime captors but I have grown used to being able to predict who I will get on each day of the week. Monsieur Grimshaw regularly draws the Thursday detention, and through my silent proximity I feel I have learnt a great deal about him. Being the first week of the month, he is equipped with the latest edition of his favoured fishing magazine. This is a publication he seems not to read, preferring instead to continually flick page after page before repeating the cycle. Depending on his level of interest, he achieves between eight and fourteen full repetitions before the cacophony of bells finally signals the end of lunch and we both shuffle back to our respective classes. On other days I have observed him with sizable television schedules, circling specific programmes with a thick highlighter pen, scientifically planning his lonely evenings, I imagine.

The use of the same room for detentions also gives the comfort of familiarity and routine and, though having over twenty desks to choose from, I always find myself positioned at the very centre of the room. Here, too, there is method to my madness. Experience has taught me that, for those detentions when I am not the sole captive, my fellow prisoners usually choose the seats by either the walls or the windows. They seek to maintain some degree of defiance and it is as though, by pressing themselves to the walls, they are able to preserve some sense of independence. Either that or achieve the maximum distance from my seemingly toxic company. Ultimately, though, the hour of detention is boring for them and, as their tolerance wanes, they inevitably look for some form of amusement, usually exercised through some small act of persecution on me or some other unfortunate. In the centre of the room, in direct line of Monsieur Grimshaw's sight, or whichever teacher is present, my exposure offers some degree of protection. Compared to the open hunting grounds of the school premises, lunchtime in detention is still relatively safe. I also sit at the centre of the room in case I feel the need to dislocate, though this on the whole just draws out the process and I have spent more than enough time in the room to retain any interest in its contents or the moribund view across the playground.

For detentions you are supposed to complete work allocated in accordance with your misdemeanour. Though, having seemingly slipped through the net and no longer recalling whose lessons I have actually missed, I have come unprepared. This is a situation I have come to learn Monsieur Grimshaw remains either oblivious or indifferent to. On past occasions I have even drawn attention to the fact, only to be greeted with an expressional shrug in keeping with his Gallic character. Though on one occasion, disgruntled at my interruption to what must have been a particularly critical analysis of the television programmes on that evening, he introduced me to what has since become one of the few repetitive behaviours I could consider constitutes a hobby.

"Colour in the letters," he had instructed, furnishing me with two felt tip pens and the back page of a broadsheet newspaper. "Alternative colours, fill in the spaces: the a's, e's, q's, o's and p's. Anything which is a complete loop."

I usually find the process therapeutic, but not today. The sickness is definitely creeping over me and I still can't keep warm. It is worse when I dislocate, something about the decay around me extenuating the battle which is now escalating within my body, turning the occasional icy shiver into violent tremors, accelerating the vague discomfort into fully blown cramps and eruptions of sticky sweat. Sitting in detention, my arms tucked under my ribs, I can smell the illness emanating from my skin, festering and percolating in the damp folds of my uniform.

I guess I could have just gone home, but this would have simply added to my considerably poor attendance record. As far as I can recall, all but a few of the absences have possessed some aspect of illness. Though this is not always specifically definable by current medical standards, I think we can all agree at this point that there is something not quite right with me.

31

Going home would have also initiated the inevitable series of telephone calls to my long-suffering parents, dragging them once more from their place of work to collect me. The stunted discussions as to my wellbeing are tiresome and at least for this hour in detention Monsieur Grimshaw allows me the seclusion I desire. I think Monsieur Grimshaw is one of my favourite teachers, though I appreciate that this might not be the case were I actually in any of his classes. My French is terrible, the spoken word being one aspect of my education that my dislocations cannot help. I consider the fact that I remain on course for a qualification in this subject as more of an indictment of the education system than a testament to my abilities.

I know letters concerning my consistent tardiness have been sent home, my parents having been summoned to discuss the anomaly which is their only child. I understand vague threats have been made as to my expulsion. But on the whole I do not fear that they will genuinely expel me, not unless I start setting fire to things or stab someone. Apart from the subsequent complications of my already fractious home life I would remain sangfroid if they had. Were it not for my indifference to my own wellbeing I might have already sought to engineer such an occurrence. Though, while my previous two schools were no better or worse than this current institution, a fresh school does offer the benefit of a small period of grace. This is because bullying takes time, a few days or weeks relatively free of physical or verbal abuse as my new classmates struggle to manifest their disgust into hatred. In the end, though, it is inevitable, observable as a creeping escalation, as I slowly replace whoever had previously held the unenviable title of most abhorrent girl in school.

But this school needs me; it certainly needs me more than I need it. Because I can tell you, without the need for modesty, my grades are good; very good in fact. Though there is an obvious reason for this which has nothing to do with my academic capabilities. I have heard

32

reference to Oxbridge whispered in hushed tones amongst the teaching staff, the first this school would have ever had. This therefore creates conflicting emotions in Mrs Jenkins, our long-suffering headmistress. On those few occasions when I am unable to avoid her I notice how her face becomes ridged, her beady little eyes become hungry as though she sees me as some sort of educational delicacy. For some reason, when speaking to me she wrings her hands nervously, though this may just be a response to my proximity. Yet I am sure, allowing the mask to slip behind closed doors, her hopes for my potential genius morph into something of a more base and practical concern. I know that the school have conducted lengthy risk assessments on me. I wonder what she would do if she suspected my intention to deliberately fail all my final exams with spectacular efficiency.

She has at least seen the wisdom to relent with the seemingly endless stream of educational and behavioural psychologists. Though I suspect her motivation is less concerned with my education or wellbeing and more due to a fear that they might terminally damage her grade averages by spiriting me away to some specialist school, hospital, or laboratory. Perhaps this is just cynicism on my part, perhaps she just has the sense to recognise that it is probably not a good idea to go looking under the rocks in my head. It is unlikely she would like what she found.

Sorry? What was that? Why was I expelled, you ask? The worrying thing is, for the first school at least, I'm not entirely sure. You have to understand that I have not been particularly stable for the past few years. The first few terms of secondary school now seem blurred in my memory.

This was a time of only limited introspection, a period of my life prior to becoming aware of, and controlling, the dislocations. It was all very, very confusing. There were a few incidents, a few disagreements of insignificance, but I struggle to associate these with the decision to expel me. The best explanation I can give is to offer the following scenario:

33

imagine yourself in a room, a seemingly normal, everyday space and then finding yourself sensing something, a noise or an unpleasant smell which, even as you concentrate, you simply cannot locate. The sensation grows, simultaneously disorientating and gripping your attention, and you begin to wander around the room in search of the source. And as you search the source remains elusive, but your frustration grows as you look under chairs, on shelves and behind curtains. From the seed of this irritation you become increasingly manic and aggressive in your struggle to make sense of your environment. Then finally there is the briefest moment of clarity, something alien which stops you in your tracks. Now, looking around the once pleasant and ordered room, you find nothing but disorder and destruction. The neat and tidy space has been decimated by your fevered efforts. It is at this moment, surrounded by the carnage of your own making, that strangers arrive. They look at you with a mixture of fear and pity. Always looking at you, as though blinkered or blind to the wreckage you have unleashed. A decision has been made, made long before they had even stepped into the room, long before they had witnessed the annihilation of your surroundings. It is at this point that you are extracted, plucked, lifted, and segregated. Now, disentangled from the disaster of your creation, you are observed in isolation. It feels wrong, but it does at least make sense. Yet the sound you were looking for still remains, like tinnitus in your ears. The smell is now saturated into your clothes.

The second expulsion, though still before my capacity to dislocate, is easily and accurately recalled. For the record, it is worth stating that I was not technically expelled. Rather, through the use of a more gentle and palatable euphemism, I was 'asked to leave'. Spitefully, I rejected this offer outright, until my ever-conscientious parents took the executive decision on my behalf. Though, as is seemingly the way with my detached existence, I could cite this institution's lack of appetite for repeated diversion from accepted norms. In accepting an 'invitation to leave', no actual justification or motive is required.

Though were one required, the list could include truancy, vandalism, disruptive behaviour, and unladylike conduct. I do not feel that my behaviour was in many ways noticeably different from that in this current place of learning. Though, undefended without my ability to excel in class due to an unfair advantage, it is understandable that less latitude was given. I wonder whether this current institution would have sought to distance itself from me had I not miraculously demonstrated a sudden ability in examinations. Ironically I have, at times, cited the additional periods of study and quiet reflection during my numerous detentions as a possible cause for my achievements. A claim which at times seems to almost retain some credibility.

VI

I blink awake to the sound of someone behind me coughing. Even without dislocating, time is being belligerent and sluggish, my sickness drawing out each nauseating second. I'm still in detention, presented with a perfect view of Monsieur Grimshaw's balding crown; possibly even the same detention I was in earlier but I can't be sure. Monsieur Grimshaw is a constant but there now seem to be other people here in the room with me and I was pretty sure I was alone when I arrived. It now seems like the weather has improved considerably, abnormally so, and I am trying to recall whether Monsieur Grimshaw was wearing a different coloured tie when I entered.

The trouble is that this is all so unsettling. As you have probably guessed I spend a lot of time here; a lot of my existence seems to be spent shuffling between identical repetitions of past experiences, constantly re-living the same scenes as though stuck in some endless looping behaviour which, over time, has lost any meaning or context. In my defence, I don't think this is entirely due to the dislocation. I am beginning to suspect that such continual repetition is just a natural occurrence and that I am in no way different in this capacity. I do not suspect that everyone else has so much difficulty with this state of affairs, though. They seemingly retain some innate capacity to not only tolerate but actively thrive in such predictable and repetitive environments. Therefore I must conclude that the only variance is my inability to cope.

Looking down, I see the front cover of a newspaper and two coloured pens, evidence that this is indeed a different detention, though it could just be the case that I have not been paying attention. That happens at times too, particularly when walking. I spend many hours wandering the various roads and alleys through my neighbourhood, but there always seem to be sizable gaps in my memory. Sometimes it is only when standing back at my front door, key in hand, that I form any conscious recollection that I have been out at all. My neighbourhood is drab and uninteresting but this in no way explains this void. There is simply so much that occurs in the average day which is done without fuss, with no conscious recognition of its importance. The most obvious of these being the inner workings of your body, but also simple mechanical behaviours are dictated and controlled as much by lingering memories in the muscles as in your constantly overworked brain.

The first column of text has been coloured, little dots of blue and green ink, giving the article the appearance of some strange technicolour braille. I am about to continue adding more coloured pimples when I'm distracted by an acute awareness of the proximity of the classmate to my immediate left. I listen as the aging desk creaks under his shifting weight, sensing the slight shift in shadows as he leans a little closer and I am certain that he is watching me. I would like to dislocate but under such close observation I fear exposure, and though I try and ignore him I find his lingering presence unwelcome and unnerving.

There is an unwritten rule concerning those sentenced to spend their lunch breaks in detention. There are numerous places in the classroom, more than sufficient to ensure that each and every one of us can serve out our sentence in relative isolation. Even my most hated of persecutors sometimes accept this unspoken agreement, allowing any latent hostility they hold against me to remain suppressed until we are released back into the wider population. This boy, however, does not know the rules and I fear his proximity is not just from a stunted sense of personal space but also that I have been specifically chosen for some unknown honour. Worse still, I can feel him watching me, not in some surreptitious, curious glance but as part of an outright overbearing study. His presence makes my sickness surge, filling my mouth with saliva and drawing what feeble strength remains from my limbs, the slightest movement now causing them to ache. He is making my head feel heavy and it is with great effort that I roll my eyes to meet, and challenge, his curiosity.

I do not know this boy. That in itself is not particularly surprising, as throughout my time in this place I have made virtually no effort to familiarise myself with any of the personal details of my classmates. Some names have somehow stuck, and others, a short list of my most ardent enemies, have become well known to me, but on the whole the vast swathes of those uniform-clad figures remain complete strangers. With most, however, I do at least retain some degree of recognition. However, this boy, even accepting mine is not the most accurate and reliable of memories, is entirely alien to me. I guess he knows me, obviously I am not popular but I am the leading champion in a small and unique cluster of freaks who have obtained a certain notoriety. A small legion of the damned, the shock troops of social ineptitude and physical repulsiveness. In this respect I am well known, the source of a collective contempt which spans all classes and age groups in the school.

I scowl at him, but to little effect. Annoyingly, he retains my gaze, disarming me with a gentle, if idiotic, grin. I have found through personal experience that my classmates are masters at engineering subtle psychological discomfort. Yet, though the effect is similar, I can detect no mischief or malice in his open, if overbearing, countenance. My resolve breaks first, locking my attention back on the coloured dots, relying on my feigned interest in my meaningless colouring to slowly break his attention span. Yet this only seems to heighten his interest in me and out of the corner of my eye I notice him rock forward on his elbows, as though watching my application of green and blue dots is suddenly some intensely interesting spectator sport.

He is a strange looking boy, a mixture of infant and adult sized features. His school uniform is worn, but far too big for him. I'm guessing the blazer is a hand-me-down from some older brother who has since been released from their academic incarceration. He has some bizarre bird's nest mop of light brown hair which sits as though knocked on a slanting angle. His soft skin gives off a sheen like polished wood and is covered in a dusting of small dark freckles. His eyes are red and I would have imagined this suggested he had been crying had he not appeared so relaxed. The eyes follow my hands with darting movements each time I reach for a different coloured pen. He is incredibly irritating, like some perverted voyeur, and it angers me that he might be deriving some warped gratification while I become the unwilling actor in some depraved fetish. The sickness comes again: a hot rippling wave of nausea. I imagine he is running some mental commentary to my every movement, some rambling monologue in hushed tones as though describing my behaviour to some enthralled third party. It is as much to suppress the trembling illness that my resolve breaks.

"What?" I ask, summoning as much venom as I can muster while maintaining a barely audible whisper. At this point the sound of Monsieur Grimshaw completing another lap of his fishing magazine diverts my attention, but at no point does he look up. The boy just shrugs, and then smiles. For a moment I am relieved that he turns the other way but this respite is only temporary. Within seconds he begins to fidget; my attention is now focused on the shifting shape at my side. It can be no longer than a minute before he is watching me once more, biting at his thick lip, craning his neck in response to my efforts to shift in my chair and turn my back on him. I can sense his interest in me, I can feel him straining to make some effort to communicate and for one horrific moment I am gripped with the fear than he might actually reach over and touch me.

"Missed one," comes the soft voice into my ear.

"What?" I ask. My question is blunt and bitter. It is though my tongue has swollen, left to laboriously flop in my mouth, making my voice sound crude and clumsy. I turn to face the boy, who is nodding eagerly. Before I can object, he leans over, causing me to physically recoil. Thankfully he makes no contact with me but still despoils my newspaper, poking at my neatly coloured dots with a soft, sweating finger. I am forced to look away in disgust from the dirt-incrusted fingernail, reeling from the warm scent of his body and liquorice.

"Look, you've missed one, here."

My blood runs cold long before the offending digit is withdrawn, dragged rather than lifted, smudging the paper with his moistness. But it is not his finger or the stain which is now the source of my bubbling horror. There, now as clear as the sun, my eyes are drawn to my oversight. Barely an inch down the first column I see the omission, the tiniest of letters, barely a space to colour in, the speck of white paper: '3rd'. Worse still, the boy continues to smile. He is nodding as though pleased with his contribution, keen to watch me complete the work I have started, casually expecting some form of gratitude for his most unwelcome of observations. It is as though he genuinely thought that he was helping me.

"You've ruined it," I spit, more out of frustration; crushed by the abject humiliation of my defeat.

Even as I say these words I realise the ridiculousness of my outrage. Yet the emotion continues to swell up, drowning my rational thought. I don't want to dislocate but my breathing is becoming jagged and strained. The sickly shivers of my illness are now gone, replaced by a high vibration of incandescent rage. I feel warm, hot even, and I suspect my sweating skin is now radiating this fury, creeping through the colour spectrum, adding what might ironically be considered to be a healthy colour. My eyes begin to hurt, my vision remains unaffected yet my mind is blind to the significance of what they see.

I am only vaguely aware of Monsieur Grimshaw looking up from his magazine, a lingering look which drives the boy's attention back to his books. Yet I find no peace of mind in the following quietness. I feel cramped and restrained by hidden forces, my muscles burn from the forced rigidity. Though, despite this, my grip continues to tighten, crushing the felt tip pen in my palm; the stabbing pain from my hand goes unnoticed. The cracked nails of my other hand now claw through the newspaper, dragging the previously smooth typed sheet slowly into ugly folds of shredding paper.

"It's OK," comes the hushed voice beside me. Even in my excessive delirium I detect a degree of concern for my spiralling loss of control. "Just colour it in now."

As a terrible, uncontrollable fear for my own safety surrounds and swallows me I know I must flee from the room. It is as though some pressing weight threatens to crush me while all the time some primitive energy risks exploding from my throat, shattering my teeth as it forces its way out of my body. For the briefest of moments, a mere flicker of consciousness, I visualise my destruction from the perspective of some third party. I watch as I lose control, twitching to the forces within me, arching my back, my head thrown violently to vent the surging powers.

"Look, let me do it."

The boy has leant over again and picked up my coloured pen. At this moment something in my head ruptures.

"No! It is ruined. It breaks the sequence. You've broken the fucking sequence!"

I don't know if it is my outburst or the muffled thud of Monsieur Grimshaw's palm against the desk but the boy freezes. Monsieur Grimshaw begins speaking, his deep baritone voice saying words I do not comprehend. Only later, I realise that it is not me he is speaking to.

"Qui êtes-vous?"

"Eh?"

"Qui êtes-vous? Quel est votre nom?"

I feel the lurch kick in my chest. As though each of my ribs seeks to stretch like fingers, forcing me to grab at my shirt to prevent them from opening my chest like a blossoming flower.

"Ah, je suis appelle Billy Rowley, sir," replies the boy. His shaking attempt at an accent disintegrates when he pronounces his name.

41

"Ah, Monsieur Rowley. Le nouvel étudiant, qui?"

"Sorry, sir?"

Grimshaw's face darkens, his narrowing eyes receding into shadowed pits. There is a deep foreboding in the room. Greater than the annoyance of a teacher torn from his reading. There is a latent horror, something that has now infected my core and threatens to obliterate everything in a three mile radius.

"Vous étudiez français, oui?"

The boy to my right says nothing, casting a hopeful glance in my direction - but I cannot hold his gaze. I border on near panic and scratch furiously, animal-like, at my naked legs. In times like these such pain gives focus.

"You study French do you not, Monsieur Rowley?" asks Grimshaw with deliberate and cold precision.

"Yes, I mean oui, sir."

My mouth is full, my swollen throat threatening to choke me. But in that moment I cannot dislocate. If anything, it is as though time is accelerating, spinning me faster and faster into some terrible void.

"And was it not during Mrs Dodd's French class you saw fit to climb out of the first floor window?"

"Yes sir."

"En français, s'il vous plaît."

"Qui, Monsieur Grimshaw."

My heart hammers furiously in my ears, a deafening, muffling thud that seems to echo in my skull. The headache is dull yet crippling, as though the pressure in my head increases, pushing against my skull, threatening to pop my eyeballs from their sockets.

"So let us seek to recoup the learning you missed during your self-administered defenestration. Tell me what happened."

"I… I climbed…"

"En français, Monsieur Rowley, en français."

"I… Je … Montee? Je…"

I only vaguely recall the boy's narrative being interrupted. A strange larynx-shredding howl, a twisted wail that rocks Monsieur Grimshaw back in his chair. The terrible noise seems to reverberate around the classroom, vibrating the windows as much as the earlier football had. There is a screech of the chair as I kick back, my hands clawing at my own throat, desperate to facilitate some erupting exorcism. Out of the corner of my eye I see the boy's face, transfixed, frozen in confusion. Only as the last of the air empties from my lungs do I realise that I was the source of the noise. For the briefest moment I am able to dislocate. But, drained and unprepared, the grinding stagnation is brief and incomplete and only moments later my burning lungs force my throat to open, sucking down volumes of gas for the next mournful cry. There is no restraint, it is like a spasm: there is a deep lurching hiccup and I spew vomit over myself and the desk, saturating the neatly coloured newspaper and broken pens in putrid acidic bile.

VII

In the dislocated world, it is easy to forget that objects remain subject to forces and, though the object might be twisted or manipulated, the vector of the force remains. Were a bullet fired from a gun, and were I able to dislocate in time, it would be in my powers to return it to the sender, rotating it to the point from where it had come before allowing it to resume its course. I have, on occasion, turned birds in flight, watching the panicked, flapping confusion as they narrowly avoid driving themselves like a spear into the ground. I have also tested the gymnastic capabilities of cats and found it quite remarkable.

My mother was deeply disturbed by the pungent stains of raw egg I had left over the carpet, unaware of the significance of my experiments in developing both understanding and control of my abilities. The test was simple enough, a small coloured cross was drawn on the shell with a marker pen, the egg then held from a height and released. Then, through a series of temporary suspensions of time, I used the position of the cross on the shell to steer my delicate cargo safely to the floor, inverting forces so that, with my final release of breath, the egg had only a fraction of an inch to fall, landing safely and without a crack or blemish. Though even this took a half dozen attempts to master, and in hindsight I could have conducted my experiments on the tiled bathroom floor rather than over the living room carpet.

VIII

"So, Francis, how is school?"

I am in Dr Attwood's office and from short sleeves and the warm easy light falling through the open windows I guess it is early summer. I vaguely recall that this session is much earlier than the one I mentioned previously. It certainly precedes the regrettable incident in Monsieur Grimshaw's detention.

Both Dr Attwood and I are in our familiar positions; she, right leg crossed over her left, slightly reclined in her expansive chair. I suspect she practices this posture to cultivate an atmosphere of openness. I, however, do not mirror this confidence. I sit bolt upright, my knees pressed together, perched on the edge of a deep cushioned chair which Dr Attwood has long since given up attempting to get me to relax into.

Here, at least, I recall allowing myself to share with her a significant degree of honesty. I tell her that school is painful and humiliating, and an experience which provides a multitude of opportunities for abuse from a number of my classmates. I tell her school is an institution in which I am forced to associate with a significant number of girls whose only similarity to me is our relative age, enabling them to compensate for their own emotional weaknesses by taking out their frustrations. Notes are taken by the eminent doctor but to no tangible benefit.

"So, Francis, what have you been doing since we last spoke?"

This is never Dr Attwood's first question; it is usually prefaced by irrelevant chitchat, but it is this question which signals the start of our sessions. I have learnt to spot the discernible shift in emphasis to the ongoing question of 'me' rather than the preamble of pleasantries. Over the subsequent months, I have become more skilled in developing an elaborate outline of what the life of a girl my age would be, were I to live it. In reality, the most accurate response to this question would be that I have spent long periods of time looking into the mirror and watching my own reflection. This was not out of vanity as I, like the doctor, have also been subjecting myself to an extensive interrogation. For I too have cause to suspect that Francis is hiding some secret from me. And like the Francis sitting in Dr Attwood's office, it took a considerable amount of time before the withdrawn figure that stared back from the mirror did anything but reiterate my questions.

The bruises point to the obvious incidents which have occurred since the last routine update of my life. That is, of course, discounting those which were self-inflicted. Due to the state of my face I can see no logic in withholding the information and I provide a detailed account of the previous escalation of physical violence from one of my regular persecutors.

"So, Francis, what have you been doing since we last spoke?"

I tell Dr Attwood that I have spent a lot of time being pummelled with ill-directed slaps and kicks while I crouch, eyes averted, braced for more significant blows. I do not, however, tell her of the revealing insight that these attacks have offered. I spare the good doctor the details of the particular event which I am sure she would only attribute to some new neurosis.

As seems to be the way with bullies, it was actually the first beating I had had for a number of weeks. It is almost like my attackers work to some secret quota system, having to build up credit to afford a more prolonged and violent attack. The periods between assaults are just long enough for me to foster the naïve hope that they might have forgotten about me. Like the repetition of Dr Attwood's sessions, there is also a certain predictability to their attacks, like some foreplay or pantomime of humiliation which we must engage in before the real business of a good kicking can begin.

The girls had been following me for quite some time, seemingly taking turns to shower me with the usual barrage of verbal abuse and mocking me with laughter. Usually, they grow disinterested long before I cross the park, which is roughly equidistant between the school and my house. I guess I could have tried to run away but this in itself is an ungainly, embarrassing spectacle. I also know that it would be a short and futile attempt at escape and it would be only a hundred yards or less before my out of shape carcass would be caught. And even if I were to somehow miraculously slip my pursuers, my escape would merely delay the inevitable by twenty-four hours, a stay of execution before they corner me in some secluded part of the school. I resent giving them the satisfaction of the hunt.

They were only a few yards behind me when I turned from the road and through the narrow alley that runs perpendicular to the neat row of terraced houses. In hindsight I question why I had taken this route, presenting my attackers with such a golden and obvious opportunity. Part of me still wonders, while being spat at and scratched, whether the attack was not subconsciously coveted. The alley is narrow and secluded and does not even lead anywhere. It seemingly has two purposes: to provide a venue for my solid beating and a place where dog owners do not have to pick up their pet's shit.

The attacks remain depressingly formulaic. Pushed against the wall, I am usually asked a repetitive series of rhetorical questions, usually goading me with some immaterial or imagined slight I may have offered. It is as though they need to warm up in advance of the assault itself, and there is no point in responding. Over the months I have tried many strategies to preserve some degree of dignity. Usually I try to either pretend they are not there or feign indifference, but nothing really works. On the whole, I have come to understand that my attackers seek humiliation more than physical harm and through obtuse attempts to rationalise their abuse or to defend myself, I am in fact just drawing out proceedings.

So with my uniform smeared in phlegm, I willingly allow myself to condense into a curled hunch, hanging my satchel across to shield my legs. I have come to the realisation that these girls are not very good at throwing punches. By dropping my chin and raising a shoulder I can, on the whole, protect my face. I allow the majority of the blows to fall across my back; they hurt and they will leave a bruise but they are ineffectual and will do little damage of significance. The kicks and stamps, however, are something different. I hang my satchel in hope of blocking them but invariably two or three precise stabbing jabs get through. They are aimed expertly, striking into the bone or joints, and there is a vomit-inducing sickness that comes with the pain. It only takes a light prod from the toe of a shoe into my shin to leave me hobbling for days.

There is a temptation at this point to drop and curl into a ball, but through bitter experience I know this must be resisted; on your feet there are limitations to the slaps and punches. They pull my hair but, despite the pain, I accept the collateral damage of whatever clumps and greasy locks come away in their fists. I tolerate this because I know that once on the floor it becomes open season. Those stinging kicks are no longer limited to calves and ankles, now free to liberally dig at hips, thighs, knees and back. While on your feet the girls seem to need to take it in turns so as not to hit each other in a cross fire. But when you are curled up amongst the dog shit, everyone can be suitably accommodated.

I cannot tell you why I did it. But, as though preparing to plunge into an icy pool, I distinctly remember shutting my eyes and tensing, holding my breath in preparation for the inevitable barrage. I guess it was just my fear that made me so unaware of what happened, the numerous injuries sustained already more than enough to distract me from the more subtle and unexpected of changes. I think it was the sound that first pricked my curiosity, the strange malodourous droning as though an old record player had been unplugged. Yet I remained restrained, cowering against the wooden fence. It was more out of confusion than hope of escape that I finally turned to face my assailants. Opening my eyes I looked up to see the world stagnating. The sound of the small mob of girls revelling in my subjugation was reduced to a low, indistinguishable murmur as the swinging arm of the nearest attacker inched comically towards my head. The girl's face was frozen in rigor mortis and hate and as I stared in disbelief I felt the soft, slow pressure of her saliva brushing my cheek. In my confusion I began to speak and the spell was broken, the arm swung, there was a ringing in my ears and my head recoiled from the impact. After what had seemed like only seconds, I suddenly found myself alone in the dirt.

IX

I don't tell Dr Attwood that I was late home that evening, the disturbing developments plaguing my thoughts as much as the memory and trauma of the attack. It was only much later, inspecting my damaged face in the mirror that I began to consider the possibility of a link between the external world and my shallow breaths. It was as though, at that moment, my illness made sense and, once aware of the misdiagnoses, from that moment the symptoms no longer unduly troubled me.

Though not as acute as at the moment of my discovery, I still find the sensation that comes with approaching the threshold of dislocation slightly sickening. It is as though, at the apex where my lungs reach their capacity, the world condenses around me and for a fleeting moment the thin air takes on a greater density. As I exhale, the fluidity returns and the experience would be easily forgotten were it not for the repetition with each changing tide of my breath.

With this cyclic motion I am restrained and released by unknown forces. I lurch through my existence, every pause and expulsion of stale gas hinting at a fundamental disparity between my organism and the powers which dictate its ebb and flow. It started as a continuous series of whispers and half glimpses of a greater truth which, until that moment, had been hidden from me. My identity was an illusion, bound tightly around me to produce the overwhelming sense of constraint, a jaded existence, swamped and suffocating.

The change is subtle but definite. From the genesis of an undefined nervous unease begins an evolution into a more physical presence of atrophy. At first it is a barely quantifiable change of air pressure and temperature on my skin, followed by a pronounced sense of fluctuation in my surrounding environment. While I perfected my abilities I tried to remain in a state of calm rigidity. The minor movements of my physical being which still occurred now seem somehow laboured, as though restrained by the increased drag of this new lipid atmosphere. Finally, as I breathed out, I became conscious of a curious resistance to the expulsion of the vapours which seeped from my mouth.

I can still clearly recall that faithful moment, standing half naked in the bathroom. I had undressed slowly, limiting the dull aches of bruises which would slowly morph through a spectrum of dark blues and purples. I allowed fingers to lightly explore the injuries, testing for pain with gentle pressure. Though the details of the attack itself were now pushed from my thoughts.

The bathroom in our house is small but it is a comforting environment. There is a small lamp over the mirror that emits a mellow yellow light, reflecting the recently cleaned porcine and softening my acne-covered features. On the other side of the door I could hear the daily life of the Kelly household, the sounds of the vacuum cleaner and the television, which resulted in the need for my parents to shout at each other from room to room.

I vaguely recall holding my breath to stop myself from crying, and I initially confused the subsequent dislocation with sickness, diagnosing the effect as some lingering residue of shock. Yet, as I exhaled and took another breath, the causality of the effect became increasingly apparent.

I had turned on both taps, allowing the water to drain through my fingers, and I became conscious of the distinct changes in texture as the mucus-like glue oozed over my skin. While the muffled noise from beyond the bathroom door offered little clue, I noticed the crisp sound of the trickling liquid became flat and droning.

With repetition, depriving myself of breath for increasing periods, I habituated to the changes, and experienced an increasingly pronounced sensation of separation. With each concentrated breath I felt the subtle changes which suggested a fundamental shift. A shift which slowly bent to my understanding and control. The separation had become a paradox, reaffirming and alienating. Simultaneously, I am withdrawn from my reality while I subconsciously impose my will upon it.

It was there, exposed in front of the bathroom mirror, that the epiphany occurred, manifesting itself in a moment of defining clarity. It was at this point, as though taking the step into the void, I drew a hard and lengthy breath and held it locked securely deep within my lungs.

X

"Eat it, Francis," my mother says.

This is the third such instruction, and irritation is beginning to creep into her voice, hinting that the limit of her patience is fast approaching. My father is also beginning to rally to her cause; he stares at me with a cool unflinching gaze, which is in stark contrast to the continuous rotating jawline of his endless chewing. Despite this, for the next few minutes, I poke suspiciously at a roast potato with the prongs of my fork. Dissecting it, before summoning the energy to prise open my jaw and allow it to close slowly around the next feeble morsel. I close my eyes as I chew, hoping that the offending object might somehow miraculously disappear, negating my need to swallow it. But the ill-defined mass remains obstinate, and it requires an almost heroic effort to empty my mouth, taking a sip of squash to signify my achievement. Through this token demonstration my mother is momentarily sated and her attention turns back to her own plate, nimbly lifting her fork to her mouth as though to demonstrate her mastery of the process.

I push peas around the plate, dividing and shifting my food as though engaged in creative accounting. The effect is to create a tepid paste that would be considered unappealing, had any appeal existed in the first place. Periodically, my mother makes observations on my progress, alternating between encouragement and veiled threats. So, over the past twenty minutes, I have made consolatory gestures, forcing as much into my mouth as any reasonable person could be expected to achieve. I have eaten to the point that, if I pile my food to one side, significant areas of the ceramic are clearly visible. Previously such an achievement would be roundly applauded by both parents but now, having raised the bar of expectation, I am instructed to clear my plate at every meal. Thankfully, the vigilance of my captors is not as manic as it once was.

53

During evening meals at the Kelly household I still find myself sandwiched between them at the dinner table, but I am no longer of such keen interest, allowing me to undergo my trials in relative peace. The lingering spectre of having to eat dessert has thankfully also been removed, my parents recognising the counterproductive nature of such threats.

It is not so much the process of consuming the food, or the biological necessity of sustenance, that I find so objectionable. Neither is it, as Dr Attwood has alluded, some sense of disgust at my physical appearance, manifesting itself in an attempt to starve my disjointed vessel into beautified submission. It is the physical act of chewing which displeases me, and I have yet to find a taste which is not deeply offensive. I find the sensation of pressing this amalgamation of substance between my teeth, and pushing it about with my tongue, little different to methodically compressing it under my armpit or allowing it to sluice between my bare toes. All of which is an unpleasant precursor to actually having to swallow the stuff, the draining repetition of each mouthful, sapping my will to continue.

Because of this, my mother has at least made some small concessions, agreeing to serve meals that are more sympathetic to my objections. We eat a lot of soups, mashed potatoes and minced meats, and vegetables are boiled to such extent that they lose all structural integrity. In the hope of taking this culinary approach to it natural conclusion, I have previously asked for my entire meal to be served to me after being blended. I have proposed, only half in jest, whether it might be possible to be forcibly fed by my father, citing the method employed on geese, to make foie gras. This was regrettably met with both disgust and outrage.

In fairness, I must state at this point, that, as far as I can tell, my mother is not a poor cook. Despite numerous other issues of contention with regards their marriage, my father has never voiced anything but compliments for the meals she serves, and routinely cleans his plate. Though I am somewhat suspicious that this may, in part, be in order to deny me a suitable example by which I might excuse myself. Part of the problem, from my perspective at least, is her puritanical effort to continually serve food which is good for me. Where, if she obtusely refuses to accommodate meals that consist of a violently imposed pulp of proteins, vitamins and carbohydrate, my favoured option would be a staple menu of processed food. Again, I must stress that this is not a result of either a preference of taste or a result of the powerful suggestion of the millions spent on advertising. Rather, it is the cold logic of a billion dollar industry that specifically caters for the immediate and seamless consumption of their product. When compared with the nutritious torment with which I must do battle most evenings, these products can be inhaled with an almost subconscious efficiency.

In addition to this, the environment of my enforced diet does not aid ingestion. Meals are spent clustered around the small kitchen table, the three chairs spaced unequally so that I am pinned into the corner, unable to escape. My father sits to my left hand side, my mother across the table from him, and this does provide useful opportunities to consider my genetic disposition.

Personally, I can see no resemblance to either of them, but I am reliably informed that I am not adopted. I share the same hair and eye colour, but this is where the similarity ends. My father possesses a muscular paunch; his continual losing battle against hair loss is currently being supplemented by a short beard and unruly ear and nose hair. My mother is a product of averages, constructed with economy; the delicate features of a small circular face sit high on a long neck, framed by a helmet of thick and unruly hair. Therefore, the blame for the unappealing assortment of parts which forms Francis must be shared equally between them.

In addition to the food on my plate, I am routinely peppered with questions by my parents, and caught in the crossfire of the functional conversations that ricochet between them. I think that, were a vote taken, both my father and I would lobby that we ate every meal in the lounge. But this is not a democracy, and such privileges are soon rescinded when my mother finds I have been discreetly hiding my meal down the sides of the sofa. Our house has a dining room, but this is reserved for special occasions, and even my mother is reluctant to create such a staid and manufactured scene. It would be a drab farce, which none of us could feasibly cope with. For some reason, meals are decreed as 'quality time' for us to spend as 'a family'. But I fear that this good intention is beginning to take a terrible toll on them, illuminating their numerous matrimonial fissures with unvarnished clarity.

At times, apart from the squeak and clink of cutlery, the Kelly family eats in silence. However, it is as though, having made ground-breaking improvements on their daughter's eating habits, my parents have begun to train their guns on other unsatisfactory aspects of my development. Now, presumably for my benefit, I am offered demonstrations of social interaction, and I am encouraged to converse on any subject of my choosing. During these charades, while struggling to grapple with the meal in front of me, my parents subject me to an array of fractured and moribund conversations. Yet, in recognising the stubborn belligerence that is their relationship, I do take a strange inspiration from their efforts, summoning the willpower to bite down on a few more mouthfuls of food.

My mother's conversations, as dinner progresses, almost become a monologue, reminding me of the one-sided narrative of the old couple at the bus station. My mother plays the role of the old woman and my father, cast into the role of Derrek, eats and mumbles laconic responses between chewing and forkfuls of food. That leaves, I guess, me as the shuffling carcass of the dog, Dorothy. But while the old woman does repeatedly address questions to the dog, as well as her husband, these are rhetorical. My mother seems to insist on a response.

"How was your day, Francis?" asks my mother. I nod a favourable, if undescriptive response.

"How was school?"

"OK," I reply, though I have little recollection of it, having spent the majority of the time hiding in the gymnasium changing rooms.

My mother sticks grimly to the task, and it is a cringe-worthy spectacle. She imposes conversation to the point that some misplaced comment or silence exposes the simmering undercurrents of our fracturing home life. Her good intentions escalate into confrontation, and then full blown hostilities. I have noticed, of late, that the arguments are becoming less frequent, but I feel this is more to do with the punch drunk weariness of the combatants than the fostering of a cordial relationship.

"Just OK?"

"Well, mum," I imagine myself saying. In this airbrushed fantasy I have both my parent's full attention. My father pauses mid-chew, turning down the television to hear my anecdote, and my mother nods encouragingly. "The day was as many others. I spent it running the gauntlet of abuse, between tedious lessons. I suppose there was one incident of note. I stole a number of sugar sachets at lunch from the canteen. Then, during my double geography class, I repeatedly spiked Mr Robert's tea, over the course of an hour."

I imagine my parents blinking with incomprehension, the food falling from my father's fork onto the dinner table with a soft thud.

"Did I not mention that I can freeze time? Oh, sorry, I guess that is an important part of the story."

"Maths was good," I reply, hoping my positive response is sufficient to terminate the conversation. I also force my face into a smile, an effort to reassure her, to offer some empathy for the futility of her efforts.

"That was excellent," says my father, lining up his cutlery to signal his satisfaction, and a sense of completion. He eats far quicker than my mother, systematically devouring each meal, oblivious to his surrounds. But now, with his plate empty, he grows bored quickly, looking around the kitchen for some other form of distraction. I, of course, am far from finished, though I suspect that my mother has deliberately sought to keep pace with my progress, as much to keep my father as a captive audience as to ensure I do not starve.

"Did you see, the council have cut down that old willow tree on Coldwater Avenue?"

"Cut down or coppiced? They trim them pretty drastically."

"No, cut down, gone completely. It was there when I went to work this morning, and now there is barely a stump. Why would they do something like that?"

"Maybe it was diseased?"

"I guess, but it looked pretty healthy to me. The street seems empty without it."

"The roots go under houses, don't they? Perhaps it was undermining a building."

There is something about the finality of my father's statement which draws a line under the conversation, and it is minutes before another topic is found.

There follows more conversations of equally insipid content, all of which wash over me as they do not require my engagement. There are comments about neighbours, a character assassination of my aunt, my father's sister, and a rendition of the numerous grievances my father has against his work colleagues and clients. This, at least, becomes animated, though my mother and I can only offer token condolences. But for the majority of the time we eat in silence, my father smothering my mother's futile efforts at dialogue with intransigence.

The lack of conversation does however give me an opportunity to study them, or more accurately, to study what, I believe, to be the impact of my toxicity. I cannot imagine that such lifeless transfers of information could have once been enough to endear them to each other. I have long since concluded that, what I witness at six o'clock each evening, is now only the decayed remains of what had once been a fevered and dynamic clash of vibrant personalities. The numerous picture frames in the house hint at such existences, but these people sitting across the table from me bear little resemblance to those young adults.

I sometimes dislocate in such moments, using the frozen snapshots to search the statues of my parent's features, hoping for the smallest hint of recognition, seeking the trapped remains of the people they once were. I look for evidence of creeping alarm at the erosion of their previous selves. I search for suggestion of some nagging doubt. I wonder whether they recognise each other, or themselves for that matter, or whether, along with the youthful spontaneity, this knowledge has also been negligently misplaced.

I would like to think that this is just the result of the inevitable onset of age and habituation, the co-dependency of their relationship, neutralising the juxtapositions of their characters. But at other times, I feel as though I must also take some of the blame. The endless exposure to the singularity of my being has dampened and supressed their dreams and enthusiasm. It is as though, through my very existence, I have picked at the stitching of their relationship and now the centrifugal forces of their hope and ambitions are slowly pulling them apart. I find myself in an unenviable position, equidistant between these drifting tectonics, able to observe, with morbid curiosity, the increasing gulf between them.

Once again the family photographs seem to lend weight to the accusation. One in particular comes to mind: a small and innocent looking image, placed discreetly on a shelf in the dining room. The photograph was taken on holiday and I guess, at that time, I was at most nine years old. I am standing in the centre, pressed between the encroaching figures of my parents. We are wearing sunhats and holding ice-cream, and all three of us are smiling. But to my discerning eye, it is clear that the rot has set in, an empty gloom that somehow seems to suck the energy and colour from the protagonists. I did this: the decay, the atrophy, the inertia. The only thing that I struggle to understand is why they have not sought to allocate blame. After all, I am admonished regularly for my appearance, my uncleanliness, my truancy, my late night wanderings, and much, much more. Yet at no point have they turned in unison to bring me to task for the irreparable damage I am doing to their lives together.

"Mum."

"Yes, dear?"

"Can I be excused?"

"You have to eat, Francis."

"But I am full, really I am."

"Eat the peas and the carrots, you can leave the rest."

I have never successfully challenged how my mother can be in a position to declare herself the appropriate arbiter of my appetite, but I have long since learnt that rational and evidence-based arguments hold little currency in such moments. Over the months and years of previous dinner table battles, I have learnt that an outright refusal to eat, or an entrenched resistance, has wider negative implications for my evening. Therefore my strategy must include aspects of genuine compliance to secure any substantial concessions.

Sometimes my father comes to my aid, scavenging bits from my plate. But not today; a withering look from my mother, reading his intentions, crushes the question before it can find utterance.

Sadly, it is probably true that this endless manoeuvring and negation is the most meaningful conversation that occurs between us. It is as though my father, having finished first, has resigned his position and declared himself exempt from proceedings. His attention is increasingly turning to the high tempo chatter of whatever sporting event is being broadcast from the television in the other room. This too I can turn to my advantage, using his restlessness against my mother, securing his unintended allegiance to draw dinner to a premature conclusion. But my mother remains a formidable adversary, and while her authority in declaring whether I am full or not is spurious, there is no denying her total dominance of the protocols of all family meals.

There is a burst of energy in the other room, the roar of a crowd that initiates the strained prose of the commentators, waxing lyrical at some vaulted act of athleticism. My father is on his feet and I seize the moment, dislocating, to scope a fist full of potato into my cardigan.

"Can I be excused?"

"No."

"But…"

"No buts, eat your peas and carrots."

I curse my mistake, feeling the warmth of the poorly chosen food through the lining of my pocket.

"But dad has…"

"Your father has eaten his dinner. He is also coming back to the table in a second."

"Yes!" My father exclaims from the other room, clapping his hands.

"But I'm missing the game."

"Francis, you hate football.

"But I…"

"Once you have eaten your peas and carrots."

My mother and I have been here before, and in such instances it must be recognised that pragmatism trumps both pride and obstinacy. So I steel myself for the final assault on my digestive system.

You would think that the prospect of freedom would help, summoning the motivation required to force down what even I now recognise to be an insignificant mass of indistinguishable sludge. But, as with most aspects of my character, there is a default rebellious position to even the most simple of instructions. The instruction triggers an innate stubbornness in my mechanism, which defies even me. Each mouthful is accompanied by the melodramatic groans of a seasoned method actress, and by the time I have choked down those last few mouthfuls, I feel as though I am at the threshold of exhaustion. I barely hear my mother's approval as I slide from my chair to trudge wearily from the kitchen.

Later, I hear the now familiar squawk and muffled growl of my parents arguing. Though I can only guess at the exchange from certain words and phrases, I am quietly confident I have once again proven to be the catalyst for the disharmony. As with dinner, it is my mother who is doing most of the talking; my father's rebuttals are forceful but laconic. Yet it is his distinctive tone which enables me to track the progression of the argument, as the two combatants move between the rooms below my feet.

If they are still bickering in twenty minutes I will dislocate to slip from the house, so if there is any meaningful resolution to any of their arguments, I am never there to see it. Though the raised voices do serve one small purpose, reminding me of the mass of potato which has now congealed in my pocket. A new and valuable addition for my collection of moulds.

XI

As a point of interest, I have made numerous attempts to determine whether there is a reverse effect to my capabilities. In that, through excited and accelerated breathing, I might be able to accelerate time, cocooning myself while the world whirls around me as though in some raging storm of relativity. I have pushed myself to headache-inducing, rib-cracking hyperventilation in order to test this theory and as far as I can determine there is no obvious effect.

From what I can imagine I don't expect that I would enjoy the sensation anyway. The agitated state of the accelerated world would batter against me and would be far from pleasant. The world is too much of a complex and frenetic place as it is and the opportunity to add to this frenzied disorder can only be a bad thing. Also, I am incredibly unfit. Anything close to laboured breath would predictably initiate an alarming increase in velocity. Running would instantly become counterproductive, as it would take me longer to get to wherever I was going. Whatever I was chasing, or more likely whatever was chasing me, would immediately benefit from my self-imposed handicap. Added to this, I imagine such abilities would serve no meaningful purpose or benefit. I would, after all, merely become statuesque while the world, oblivious to my ponderous observations, would just hurry around me. The only potential benefit I can think of would be to skip through periods of my life which are otherwise dead time.

But even this is worthless to me, because I can honestly say that I never get bored. Even before I developed the capacity to dislocate my tolerance for inactivity and uneventfulness was extensive. Both my parents, my teachers, and Dr Attwood seem to consider this to be another alarming trait, but I would argue that they are overlooking certain fundamental benefits that such abilities offer. I think the rationale is inherently flawed. They erroneously consider my acceptance of the mundane to represent an 'inability' to become bored. Following this train of logic they have also seemingly begun to question whether I genuinely possess any discernible interests, and consider my absence of boredom merely a symptom of my stunted capabilities. This is unfair; I have a great number of interests. The problem comes primarily in that the things that interest me just happen to be things in which the vast majority of my peers not only do not share, but also seem entirely oblivious to.

By way of example, just this morning I spent a considerable amount of time racing raindrops. A momentary event you would think, but when experienced through an enhanced dislocated state, the descent of these two droplets of liquid down a sheet of glass becomes a true test match of seemingly limitless possibilities. It is a race filled with symbolism and metaphor. Two rain drops, indistinguishable even to my heightened sense, beginning their journey high on the window pane. Yet the meandering path they take, forming alliances with other droplets, their fortunes buffeted by favourable or ill winds, is a pure expression of the fickle nature of fate. As to why droplet 'A' swiftly gathers speed while droplet 'B' merely grows bulbous is a mystery. Why droplet 'C' suddenly stops barely inches from the finish line to allow droplet 'D' to slowly creep past it has filled countless hours with endless speculative theory.

The large patio window in the dining room is best for these titanic battles but this unfortunately does mean a loss of privacy. The garden onto which the patio leads is overlooked by windows of a number of my neighbour's houses, and I can appreciate the concern my behaviour might evoke in the casual observer. Similarly, those in the house can have little comprehension of what I am looking at. I know that it distresses my parents, watching the catatonic image of their daughter staring out expressionlessly onto the wet and wind-swept garden for hours at a time, slowly, like some reverse ascent of man, dropping into a crouch. The final exhilarating finish occurs barely inches above the carpet. As such, I usually watch from the privacy of my bedroom.

This is even better than my other pastime of confusing insects. I foolishly mentioned this to Dr Attwood and it annoyingly became the focus of a number of our sessions. I suspect she believes this to be some manifestation of some latent sadistic tendency. No matter how many times I correct her, she continually brings up the issue of pulling wings off moths or burning ants with magnifying glasses. At times I think it is the good doctor who may be suppressing rather unsavoury personality traits. To avoid the tiresome repetition here I will state now, for the record, that I do not torture or kill insects. Or any animal for that matter. There are a few exceptions, but on the whole I like all animals and it is also true that I find their company vastly superior to that of humans.

Bamboozling a dog is, of course, very easy. You simply pretend to throw the ball and don't let go; the look of wonder on the mutt's face is only cheapened by being so easily achievable. Through dislocation I have found you can freak out cats very easily, though I don't do this very often as it is clearly distressing for them. Insects, however, are much harder to assess. Confusing insects is something different, dislocation allowing me a degree of intimacy and manipulation which I suspect an entomologist would kill for. The main point is ultimately to try, with any degree of confidence, to manage to instil any degree of bafflement at all. I suspect a moth batting against a light bulb might be confused, or a fly buzzing angrily against a glass window. But how can you tell?

Just because these pastimes do not bore me, it does not mean I am incapable of such a state. Though I do still struggle to see why I should need to justify this trait. I am of the opinion that I *could* get bored. I think that if you placed me in a small box, and were feasibly able to feed, water and clean me without drawing too much attention, I might very well grow exceedingly bored in well under a year. Possibly after only a few months.

Such a tolerance for the mundane is also exceedingly useful when you have been kept off school following being violently and hysterically sick while colouring in a newspaper. The obvious benefit of being kept off school is tempered by being confined to one's room. It is not the room itself or even the quarantine I dislike. I am quite happy to sit here, but I do find, while seated in this room, that I feel like an imposter.

Each morning I wake to find myself maintaining a fraudulent existence, surrounded with various props to reflect what Francis Kelly would surround herself with were such trinkets to hold any meaningful value. My bedroom is a curious place, filled with objects which are technically mine but evoke no sense of association. Sometimes I do look through the drawers and examine my various possessions, turning them over in my hand as though trying to fathom their purpose. Many are now considered entirely inappropriate for a girl my age to still be interested in. But these relics of my infancy do at least still retain the residue of proper memories and interaction. This is a ball, I tell myself, squeezing my fist around the tooth-marked toy. I played with this, I bounced this ball, and I watched it roll. This was an object which once entertained me. I recognise the narrative but cannot fathom as to how this was ever possible.

The later additions, those deemed relevant to a fourteen-year-old girl, were on the whole impressed upon me by my parents. It is as though, in offering these gifts, they are seeking to ignite some dampened and suppressed personality. I try not to hurt their feelings while going to great lengths to avoid fostering expectation or encouragement. I take them graciously as a visiting dignitary might take some bizarre totem of some obscure culture, storing them out of sight at the earliest possible opportunity. I sometimes feel like this room is a store room, the possessions are stacked on shelves and in cupboards, waiting for the elusive Francis Kelly to arrive and take ownership of them. Mr and Mrs Kelly have bought all the equipment, now they just need the daughter to go with it.

I do have a fair number of books and this is an acceptable interest, even if I am colouring in the loops rather than reading them. These now stack up on the floor and the window ledge and their primary purpose is to increasingly block out the light. It is more the general state of disorder than any particular object which dominates the room. There are numerous cups and bowls which, over time, have morphed from drinking receptacles into makeshift petri dishes; dirty coffee cups and abandoned glasses of tepid water, which are now beginning to jaundice with yellowish tints. I grow moulds. Well, that is not true, moulds grow and I do not prevent them, so white furry spores blossom from green and purple patches. I also have the habit of hoarding food and then forgetting about it. The location only subsequently identified as the remains of whatever it was I had hidden becomes so wretched and rancid that even I have to remove the offending article. That I seek to stockpile these food stuffs is strange even to me, as I rarely have any intention of eating what I take from the kitchen.

My parents, particularly my mother, rage against my unkempt state constantly, and in my defence I do periodically purge this living space. On the whole, it is not the refuse which is removed but whatever minor trinkets may have come into my possession and of which I have since lost interest. Invariably some of the rubbish is swept away in such instances. These purges occur approximately every two months. This is another issue which is of constant interest to Dr Attwood and my mother. I suspect they think this is simply stubbornness on my part, that I may be doing this out of spite.

That I am not a tidy person is a factor my long-suffering parents continually attribute to the plethora of alternating physical illnesses, complementing the malaise of the psychological diagnosis. Yet I feel comfortable and content in my squalor, creating a suitable environment to suit the biologic mass which is Francis Kelly. Surrounding myself in growth and decay I can almost feel a sense of belonging. In the slowly settling dust and the germinating moulds, I have found something that shares the glacial pace of my dislocated existence.

Though my temperature broke over the weekend, my parents have mercifully offered a brief stay of execution from my return to school. Even here there was conflict, my father's concerns over my continual absence being tempered by my mother's pride in having such an academic child. Again, were it not for my considerable, and illusionary, prowess in my studies I labour under no misapprehension of being given such latitude. She knows I have a test this week but I have been able to impress on her the value of rest and relaxation over last minute revision. Despite this, I have already decided that I will only manage a respectable score. The test is, after all, of no real importance and it is not advisable to always maintain such consistently astounding results.

Therefore Monday came and went, the majority of the time spent forming condensation from my breath on the window or exploring my dislocated world. I have rarely left my room all day and though my bedroom door remains firmly shut, I listen to my mother as she moves about the house.

However, when the doorbell chimes at quarter past four it triggers some innate dread. Suppressing this strange tension, I slowly open the curtain but the angle to the front door is too steep and the unknown intruder is already inside. Instead, I open the bedroom door, creeping to the top of the stair to eavesdrop on the conversation. I hear my mother's voice first, laced with confusion and scepticism. Then I hear another voice and my chest tightens in horror. It is him, the boy. I neither know how he has found me nor for what vendetta he continues his strange grinning pursuit.

"Francis, honey, you have a friend."

I recoil back from the banisters, seeking out a suitable hiding place. My first choice is to hide in the bathroom, but this is swiftly rejected as an unescapable dead end. My bedroom is rejected through similar reasoning.

"Francis. Billy Rowley is here. He has brought you some books from the classes you've missed."

My initial reaction is to scream down the stairs that he is a liar. But as I lean forward I stop myself. As far as I can recall this boy is in none of my classes but I suddenly find myself unable to bring to mind the face or name of a single boy who is. I am forced to concede that those faceless uniforms are a complete mystery to me, those rows of desks that lay behind my chair at the front of the classroom are as alien to me as distant planets.

"Francis!"

I shut my bedroom door and step backwards, retreating into my parent's room. I concentrate on my breathing, preparing for the opportune moment. My mother calls out to me again and I listen to the soft footfall as both she and the boy climb the stairs. My mother is engaging in bland banter with this intruder, she is gabbling nervously and, I suspect, is excited and relieved at the revelation that her daughter is not the alienated loner that numerous professional doctors have certified. She has ushered him through the house like some visiting royalty or foreign ambassador. The boy is answering her questions with faithful humility, painting exactly the portrait that will appeal to my mother. Even in this moment I fill with the dread of the countless questions she will be peppering me with over the coming days and weeks.

"Francis, please come out here, darling."

But I am patient. Only when I hear the pronounced rap of knuckles against my bedroom door do I take the sustained draw of breath, sensing the now familiar constriction of time and molecular atrophy. Finally I peek around the door. The statue of my mother has her fist raised to the door, the boy, he seems smaller than when I last saw him, stands post-like, the numerous tattered textbooks still hugged across his pigeon chest. I duck my head back behind the wall and breathe out and in once more.

"Frannccccciiiiiiii......"

By the time my mother's voice has droned out I peer round once more. In that single second both statues have shifted. They have moved only small amounts but this is now enough to create a clear tunnel, wide enough for me to slink through the gap without touching them. This is not entirely necessary. I could, if needed, clamber over both of them and they would remain oblivious to my intrusion. My lung capacity is more than sufficient to ensure I am safely free from the house before being forced to exhale. The problem comes from the collapsing void of my wake. The faint yet detectible whisper of breeze that hints at my secret passage.

Though they remain ignorant of the true cause, both parents have frequently commented on how draughty our house is. It is almost comical to observe their bafflement. The building is modern, less than ten years old, yet despite the expensive double glazing, new doors and numerous padded draught excluders, it remains as windswept as some medieval castle. My father has joked about the house being haunted. This is not a comment appreciated by my mother, the prospect of adding possessions and exorcisms to my list of ailments and treatments is seemingly too much to bear. Ultimately, it is prudent to not risk raising their suspicions.

I squeeze through the space, contorting so as to pass with minimum disruption, before stepping into the bathroom. In the moment between breaths I hear another light rap on my bedroom door. But once time has condensed, I step out once more onto the landing.

The boy's head has turned as though tracking my escape and for a brief moment I feel a pang of fear at the possibility he can detect my dislocation. Yet, like my mother's, his features are rigid and unresponsive. The stare is absent, almost wistful. I would like to stay longer, use my advantage to sift through his pockets in search of clues as to why he is hounding me. But my abilities remain limited and I choose discretion over valour, fighting my way down through the soup-like atmosphere of the staircase.

In the hall I pause once more and listen to the sound of the door being opened. The idea of this boy in my room suddenly offends me, and while I prepare for another dislocation I visualise him touching those things which clutter around my bed. Why this disgusts me I do not know. Were these objects hurled from the window to be set on fire on the front lawn I would not lament their loss. Yet to have this boy touch them seems like some abhorrent contamination. And though the room is far from being considered a sanitary environment, it is the presence of this boy which represents an intolerable pollutant. For a brief moment I even consider going back upstairs, challenging him, dragging him first from the room and then from the house. I feel my sickness return. The faint shudder and head swim as though it is this boy who is the catalyst of my illness. It had been my intention to spy on their conversation but now this recurrent malady makes my decision for me. Under the cover of another strained dislocation I flee from the building, not bothering to close the door behind me. The narrow path which runs behind my house shields my escape, allowing me to storm anonymously away in disgust.

XII

By now I am sure you have noted some glaring contradictions in both my thoughts and behaviour, the various discrepancies that float to the surface the more we stir and sift through the ramblings of this internal monologue. I am tempted to apologise, but I am not sure that this is appropriate or justified. I feel that this might just be what is required, and these fundamental discrepancies serve to illustrate the point more accurately than my laboured and stuttering narrative. Perhaps this is the point of it all, to unroll this intricate tapestry of oxymoron, juxtaposition and paradox. Now you, like me, can look at Francis Kelly in her entirety, look at what she is, see how she is built and scratch your head at the endlessly shifting labyrinth of conflicting drives and forces. Like me you might just throw your hands up in incredulous wonder at how something so fundamentally flawed could have possibly even be considered, let alone permitted. All I can do is to say that I have resigned myself to the absurdity of this creation. I have accepted the ridiculousness and complexities in so much as they are familiar to me and each in their own right has become the exception which has proven some other rule.

XIII

I have worked myself into a state again. My thoughts become repetitive, endlessly turning in on myself, simultaneously blaming me and casting me as the downtrodden victim. At one point I find myself pacing, manically walking in figure of eight circles, mumbling under my breath while my animated hands gesticulate to the raging debate in my head. I have made a conscious decision to try and avoid creating such spectacles. Worse still, in my flight I have forgotten my coat and within minutes the cold is leeching into my bones and threat of the sickness returns, forcing me to turn back. It is like suffering further insult to the injury. Thankfully, the boy is gone by the time I slip back into the house and I stay just long enough to retrieve my coat and drop the offensive school work into the kitchen bin.

At times like this I find petty criminal acts do wonders for my sense of control and self-esteem. I must confess that once achieving a certain mastery of my abilities there was a significant spike in shop thefts, but I rarely steal from shops anymore. Perhaps, on occasion, I take the odd chocolate bar, but otherwise my tastes are sufficiently stunted to render their precious wares safe from my time-distorting fingers. What's more, the exhilaration of the first theft has never since been satisfactorily replicated. Even though, in hindsight, it was a small and insignificant robbery.

Yet I was pleased with the logical planning with which I approached the robbery: this was no opportunist, clumsy grab for the most easily available prize. The shop was chosen due to my familiarity with it and the fact that, as far as I am aware, it is not suitably equipped with closed-circuit television. This was a primary concern - video evidence of the flickering instance of my dislocation might make interesting viewing to the eagle-eyed.

"Good morning," barked Mr Ng. A product of his enthusiastic use of limited English. He is a nice enough man, I guess. Certainly having done nothing to justify losing his morning's float in an instant

I, of course, smiled and wished him a good morning, sliding the sweets and the exact change towards him, dropping a few coins on the floor at the moment he opened the till, conveniently ducking out of his line of sight beneath the counter. It takes but a moment, if such a thing exists, for the scene to solidify, my depleting air supply offering more than enough time to duck under the counter and have my choice of Mr Ng's takings. While I'm there I take some cigarettes and momentarily flick through the top pages of the adult magazine strategically hidden from view of his customers. Only one object gives me any cause for consternation. There is a wooden bat wrapped in industrial tape hidden below the counter. It is a product which alludes to Mr Ng having been subjected to less subtle and skilful robberies in his career as a shopkeeper.

Back in my crouch below Mr Ng's counter, I breathe out and there is a moment of anxiety as to whether the missing wad of notes might be instantly recognised. But I hear the till slam shut and stand up to the beaming features of his small, circular face, happy with the outcome of his latest transaction. I say my goodbyes and catch a glimpse of the watery reflection of Mr Ng waving me goodbye in the shop window as the doorbell chimes above my head.

But the intensity of that moment faded quickly, and I had barely walked one hundred yards before the significance of my crime had almost slipped entirely from my thoughts. Then, when I looked down at the wad of purple and brown notes crushed into my hand, they seemed little more than meaningless strips of paper and I could not think of a single thing I wished to buy with them. For all intents and purposes, my pockets might as well have been stuffed with empty crisp packets or toilet paper. And as soon as I was struck by this epiphany

74

my new wealth became a burden to me, just something else which failed to instil any excitement or meaning. Just another example of my incompatibility, a benchmark by which my corrupted state had inherently severed me from my peers. I carried my ill-gotten gains around with me for the majority of the afternoon. But the truth was this was simply because I had forgotten about it, only recalling the crumpled ball of printed paper when I absentmindedly stuck both hands deep into my pockets on some other errand. It was mere coincidence that I found myself standing on the narrow cycle path over the motorway at the time. But the location was convenient, enabling me to dispose of my new found fortune, as I stood tearing each note neatly in half and posting them through the chain mail fence. There was something satisfying about not even bothering to watch as they were carried away by the wind, buffeted by the thundering buses and cars. But I think this was more due to the sensation and sound of the ripping notes than any symbolism of the shredded wealth fluttering and swirling into the early evening gloom.

Such rebellious endeavours remained a distraction for a few more days, but I could already sense that my heart was not really in it. The thefts became compulsory, swift, and sometimes subconscious. In the final analysis I must conclude that these were crimes which only momentarily jerked me from my ambivalent state. I sought more daring crimes but these ultimately only served to undermine my flagging enthusiasm for my fledgling criminal career. The robberies themselves simply becoming elaborate, high risk games of hide and seek in which jewellers and museums were ultimately liberated of various curiosities. The only outcome I now look back on with any great degree of satisfaction is that the discovery of my activities made our local newspaper, many of the missing artefacts turning up when the local council dredged a stagnant duck pond.

I have not raised the point with Dr Attwood but, were I inclined, I feel I could offer a defence of my state of mind. Ironically, when you discount the continual abuse and beatings,

I am inherently satisfied, maintaining a vague state which may even border on contentedness. This is primarily because I am, in the main, impervious to the lures and insecurities associated with the trappings of material wealth. This is not a product of a rejection of materialism or some resounding inner confidence. It is now, when I consider the ease with which objects and money are obtainable, all things have effectively lost the veneer of whatever illusionary value they may have previously clung to. They have become, at best, purely functionary.

Clearly, when relating to stealing from shops, my capabilities are still limited to relatively small items. Yet this would not prevent me amassing a significant sum of money. However, at no point have I sought to accrue and stash my swag with the intention of greater or grander purchases. As I have no use for them. If you consider the cost of a car, buying one would be even more difficult than stealing it. Once you also factor in my inability to drive and having nowhere meaningful to go, the whole debate becomes mute and theoretical.

Stealing from people, however, remains a lingering habit. I am pretty indiscriminate in my choice of targets and entirely without ethical consideration for my victims. I am certainly no champion of the people as, if there is any resemblance of a modus operandi, I do have a tendency to steal from buskers, charity collections and beggars. Other times it is they who benefit from earlier crimes, and on more than one occasion I have received significant thanks for giving back the same money I had taken from the same individual just moments before. For the sake of symmetry, and as way of mitigation, Mr Ng has also found himself to be both victim and benefactor.

I guess I do it primarily because it is so easy, merely having to bend down and pick up the money. But it is not necessarily the openly displayed money which singles out those who I target. Sometimes it is just that something about a particular person interests me and, while dislocated, I rummage through their bags and pockets, liberating them of whatever trinkets momentarily spark my curiosity. Their wallets are the primary target but, as I have already said, the money does not interest me. Rather, it is everything else that holds my attention. The photos of partners, children, and pets can tell you a lot about someone, as can the various receipts, business cards, and expired club memberships.

Strangely, while indifferent to money, I am drawn to coupons and vouchers. There is something about those coloured scraps of paper that appeals to me, but why this is the case I can't really explain. I could if I wanted quite easily steal the vast majority of things that are offered but I retain no interest in them. Yet when armed with a voucher, a stolen voucher at that, the same object does suddenly have some curious allure. But in most instances, for the statues which become the focus of my interest, I rarely take that much. Having satisfied my curiosity this is, on the whole, sufficient to spare them any significant financial loss. That is not to say they may not find themselves inconvenienced as I do have an unsavoury habit of subsequently dropping their credit cards down drains or burying them in flower beds.

Of course, they all possess mobile phones, car keys, and pens, but these rarely interest me. The phones are always locked. Yet it is quite surprising just how unexpected and diverse the range of objects in people's pockets can be. Some of them are so alien and unexpected as to hint at intriguing anecdotes, leading me to subsequently follow them for a number of hours in the hope of learning more as to how such a bizarre thing found its way into their possession. Yet these are very rare occurrences; in the main I am sadly disappointed at the distinct lack of imagination of my momentary catatonics.

At other times it is they who are the benefactor, but I can only imagine their confusion when they finally discover whatever gift it is that I have seen fit to bestow on them. Some afternoons I can spend hours lifting some small token from one person's pocket, simply to deposit it in another's. In most instances I choose the objects which are worthless or meaningless and I suspect that the vast majority never even notice, let alone give more than a moment's consideration, to my small interventions. But the next time you stick your hand in your pocket and find a pen lid, small stone, or a spare button you do not recognise, it would give me a moment's pleasure if you paused to consider whether I, or someone like me, may have been at work. On reflection this behaviour seems arbitrary even to me, and if there is a method or some perverse motive I am not sure I am aware of it. Perhaps it is just that I am standing too close, unable to see the entirety of my plan. But more likely, I fear I must concede that there is no higher purpose to these trivial interventions.

I also enjoy stealing mail, loitering in anticipation of that fraction of a second when the postman leaves either their van or the post box unguarded. Unfortunately, people don't write many personal letters anymore but I still obtain considerable insight into the sheer quantity of tedious correspondence which bounces back and forth. It is quite insightful to see just how meaningless the majority of it is. Through the few handwritten letters which do still circulate, I have gained a significant percentage of my tenuous understanding of social interaction. Yet through this I have come to realise just how stunted some people's abilities to communicate are, leading me to question whether such an unbridgeable gap between the general population and myself truly exists. On the whole, I find their comments so formulaic, perfunctory and predictable that I wonder why they ever bothered sending the letter at all.

Birthday cards are the worst. In a card already bearing the words 'HAPPY BIRTHDAY', I am surprised just how many simply repeat this statement in their own handwritten note, and sign. Anniversary and get well soon cards are little better. It seems that only those letters which acknowledge life and death, letters expressing deepest sympathy or the birth of a new baby, can draw anything close to meaningful expression. Whether these sentiments are genuine and heartfelt I could not tell you.

All in all, when considering the powers at my disposal, I hope you will agree that the sum total of my criminal enterprises are both modest and restrained. While this is primarily due to the nonpartisan attitude to both personal wealth and the swarming bipeds which intersect my path, there is also still the lingering fear of exposure. Not so much a fear of the police or a prosecution for my crimes but the threat of wider awareness of my capacity to dislocate. It is the threat of a deeper and more hostile scrutiny to that of Dr Attwood which I fear, the possibility that I might find myself under a much more invasive and dissecting microscope of scientific interest. A lung full of breath can only place me at a certain distance from the scene of any incident. The potential that some careless moment or unforeseen observer might witness the before and after effects of my transition is a constant concern. I fear that it is simply impossible that such abilities, even those as clandestine as my own, will remain undetected forever.

I guess at this point I should also admit to, alongside the various thefts, a discreet number of pranks and practical jokes. Though on the whole these have not been malicious or particularly destructive. I cannot lie; in the past they have occasionally resulted in some small acts of humiliation, but do not endanger my stunned mannequins once time is reinstated. But as with the prospect of great financial gain, my interest in such exhibitions was short-lived and half-hearted in nature. As I have said before, I am not, on the whole, a violent person.

I know what you are thinking. Well, we'll get to that.

XIV

It is hard to explain what it is like when you dislocate. The best I can offer is to say that I sense the changes as the world and I separate along two distinct paths of normality. The universe grinds to a mechanical halt, stagnating at a molecular level. Initially, this evokes a sense of restraint but this claustrophobia soon erodes and is replaced with a liberating feeling of escape, a freedom not only from my personal limitations but also the very fabric of the physical world. And with this change I gain insight into the true nature of time: that the laws of physics are just arbitrary rules to an insignificant game which I can choose to no longer adhere to. By training myself to hold my breath for longer and longer periods I begin to realise my potential. With focus and concentration, a fraction of an instant's controlled restraint can bring the very structure of existence to a seamless, decaying halt. With repetition, my breath control improves, and as it improves I refine the ability to shrink further from the constraints and dependency of the world around me. It is as I approach the point of absolutes that I am able to observe the impact and implications I have on my environment.

I can best describe the dislocation as an alignment between my emotional state and the physical world. It is as if the world has finally acknowledged that I do not belong within its confines and makes the necessary concessions required to expel me. I become cocooned, much like the irritating grain of sand in an oyster, encased to remove its abrasive effect. I become imprisoned in a virtual, three-dimensional photograph. My body compensates for the complete absence of sound from the external world and I become acutely aware of the cardiac drumming in my chest. Even if I violently pound my fist against upturned surfaces, this muted environment does not respond.

There is no such thing as space in a world where time has stopped at a molecular level; every stationary airborne particle hangs at rest in the elemental soup which is our planet's atmosphere. I feel the cold of the microscopic sheen of vacuum I have instantaneously created, but I retain the warmth of my own homeostasis. At first, the effect seems quite pronounced but this swiftly passes. There is a momentary spike in temperature, comparable to a sickly shiver, as though passing from synthetic air-conditioning into the oppressive heat and humidity before a violent storm.

It is only when I move that I begin to comprehend the scale of the transformation I have instigated. The static atmosphere becomes increasingly resistant to my physical movements as my body serves as a plough, condensing billions of stationary atoms, creating areas of pressure and localised vacuums in the space my body sweeps clear. As a result, increasing effort is required to move in each direction, shunting the molecules into a dense fold, like bunched fabric. To overcome this resistance I have learnt to tack like a ship, rotating my hips and rolling my shoulders. I am required to crouch, bob and side step in order to seek low pressure. Over time my 'dance' has become quite elaborate. I liken these twisted and lithe contortions to some disjointed jellyfish that bends and arches its brittle form. Like cascading water I seek the path of least resistance and on occasions I have mocked the absurdity of this hidden spectacle, confident that, were my class mates to ever see it, it would be guaranteed an additional savagery to my next beating.

Behind me, I leave a vacuum tunnel of lurching humanoid motion and when I finally exhale the world inhales behind me and I feel a faint cold breeze across my body as the balance is restored. Ultimately, the dislocation is only as prolonged as the burning constriction of my lungs will allow. As I exhale the imposed inertia implodes, whiplashing me back into the equilibrium of the world around me. But there is no pain, there is hardly any physical sensation at all, rather a feeling of a sudden awakening, like the opening of closed eyelids to a brightly lit room following a prolonged period of absolute darkness.

The slide towards dislocation and complete inertia is steady. But, as my control grew, I found I could control the trajectory of time's arrest. If required, I can bring the world to a shuddering halt in only a fraction of a second, yet I can also induce a moribund fluidity, allowing time to decay into suspended animation. Yet without the noticeable passage of time my senses lose their point of reference. The world I perceive is reflected by the increasing urgency and palpitations of my lungs and heart. The only measurement of time is the falling level of oxygen in my bloodstream.

XV

The male police officer lets me sit in the front passenger seat of his patrol car while his female colleague speaks with members of the ambulance service. Despite the door having been open, the heater is on and the car warms up quickly, inducing waves of weariness. The vehicle smells like it has recently been cleaned, a blend of citrus and pine. My eyes scan the interior for clues about the driver but I find nothing of interest. Checking down the side of the seats and the ashtray I find none of the usual assortment of mislaid possessions, such as the loose change and sweet wrappers that amass over time in my father's car. I dislocate quickly to take a peek into the glove compartment but there is little of interest. I had hoped for some handcuffs or a gun but find only a dog-eared log book and a half used can of de-icer. There is no stereo in the car; in its place sits an intriguing collection of police equipment: display screen and illuminated buttons, which have been built into the dashboard. I have to fight to restrain the temptation to begin pressing these buttons. I have identified which one is the siren and my finger hovers precariously above the button. I doubt it would constitute a criminal offence to press it, but would certainly endanger the previous goodwill of the officers.

Due to the early hours, neither the patrol car nor the ambulance has its flashing lights on anymore. This is a shame as I had enjoyed the certain notoriety that my presence in this car would have caused to the casual observer. The revolving blue lights had also produced an interesting strobe effect, illuminating the various trees, shrubs, and manicured front lawns with a ghostly pallor, creating rapid, flickering shadows - and the phosphorus flashes as the light reflects from the windows of darkened rooms. Now, only the yellow glare from the vehicle headlamps produces deep shadows, and the warm glow from the back of the open ambulance provides me a view of the various equipment and the single old man wrapped in a blanket. On their arrival, the flashing blue lights had energised the otherwise sleeping street.

Yet most of those drawn out from their houses had now been beaten back by their lethargy and the cold. Though up and down the street I see that many lights are still on in the houses. Occasionally I see a curtain twitch.

The officer will drive me home shortly but there is no sense of urgency. Surprisingly enough, I have neither been in trouble with the police nor come to the collective attention of the authorities outside the medical profession and Social Services. Fortunately, I am not in trouble now and both the police and the ambulance driver have been nice to me. No doubt I will be in trouble later when I return home at four o'clock in the morning in the back of a police car, but I doubt that my parents will be surprised. My nocturnal ramblings remain the source of many arguments but I feel that both of my parents are now resigned to my inevitable escapes. Yet I am usually home by this hour and I can imagine the degree of unease that such an early morning telephone call from the police will induce.

I awoke and slipped through the house about three hours ago, the alternative being to lie wide awake, staring blankly at the ceiling above my bed, allowing my brain to run rampant through a lengthy sequence of ill-advised ideas. Dr Attwood says that I am an insomniac but I disagree and think she is looking for symptoms for a condition which is simply not there. The truth is that I simply do not need that much sleep; two to three hours a night is seemingly more than sufficient to enable me to endure the following day. I rarely, if ever, struggle to go to sleep if I wish to. The dislocations help, providing a stagnant, fatigued environment which seems naturally disposed to conjuring the sleeping state. My sleep is shallow and dreamless, sometimes skimming the surface of an empty consciousness.

This issue repeatedly comes up in my therapy sessions and Dr Attwood regularly asks me about how much sleep I am getting. Yet I don't see why I should need to explain or justify why my circadian rhythms do not work to the standard human cycles and I am also not sure why she should be surprised by this eventuality. I yawn occasionally, and Dr Attwood

84

rarely fails in giving this as evidence of my sleep-deprived state. I have in the past pointed out that her office is usually very warm and, while not meaning to be rude or upset the doctor, these sessions are becoming increasingly repetitive.

In previous sessions Dr Attwood has also explored the possibility that I might be sleep walking. This theory at least seems interesting, but regrettably this is not the case. I understand that I have sleep walked in the past, having been found by my parents on numerous occasions in my infancy silently ambling through the various rooms of the house. But even these were just isolated incidents and I have been led to believe such occurrences are not entirely uncommon in children. In hindsight I accept that this may have just been one of the first hints that all was not well with Francis Kelly. I suspect that Dr Attwood thinks this too and now just uses these questions to disguise the thrust of her genuine lines of enquiry.

With regard to my current night time wanderings, I concur that I frequently return home with very little conscious recollection of where I have been, or for how long I have been walking. This, however, is merely the product of the fact that there is rarely anything happening near where I live at three in the morning and because I am thoroughly habituated to my surrounding neighbourhoods. Some nights I can walk for many miles and anyone who walks for pleasure can tell you that, as one foot falls in front of the other, the internal monologue rarely comments on the immediate surrounds unless provoked by a passing car or the fleeting silhouette of a cat.

The neighbourhood becomes my own at night, the darkness providing the welcome cloak of impunity. Before it became too cold I used to like riding my bicycle; something about the darkness and cool air gives an enhanced sense of speed. That I used to do so without any lights was yet just another thing for my father to worry about. He made me promise not to, but we both knew I would not keep my promise. It is for this reason I feel he is being tardy in fixing the punctured tyre for me.

The early morning is like an approximation of the dislocated state. There is movement, but time is your own with the additional benefits of the ease of manoeuvrability. The summer nights are more pleasant for walking but rarely allow the same degree of exclusivity as the colder months. A winter's night after a fall of snow is the best, the biting elements creating a welcomed hostility. The suffocating frozen blanket grinding the mechanics of my town to a halt, covering the ugly blemishes of human endeavour. The wind only adds to this forlorn emptiness, a perfect white canvas for me to leave the brief and vague marks of my footsteps.

There is always traffic but at that hour of the morning there is sufficient time to consider each vehicle in detail and I find myself wondering what trial or labour has forced those poor souls from their beds at this ungodly hour. Occasionally, you meet the passing stranger but I always dislocate to avoid them. This is not out of concern for my personal safety, but I cannot deny I feel unease in having to share my silent world. There is a bristling danger to these figures, these alternative versions of myself, evoking a natural tendency to view them as unwelcome, if not hostile. They challenge my dominance of these streets, corrupting their unblemished, deserted state.

I prefer my silent, darkened world, free of the clutter of humans and their emotions. The houses are black boxes, mausoleums, their slumbering occupants blissfully unaware of my silent passage. On the whole, I keep to the residential areas. The factories work through the night and those few shops and public houses, though shuttered and closed for the night, still draw the remanences of humanity. What little that happens at three o'clock in the morning happens for obscure reason. It is as though events occur in isolation and without the corrupting and confusing chaff of daylight trivialities. They are stripped bare and exposed in their uniqueness, allowing the patient observer greater insight than they would ever have intended.

Such was the case in point of the solitary figure I observed loitering on the corner of Casewick Avenue and Hambridge Road. It was clear that everything was wrong - he stood and dithered, neither waited nor walked. His nervous fidget and short stuttering steps suggested he was scared to step from the curb. Until that point I had been casually sauntering down the centre of the street, only on one occasion having to step between parked cars for the solitary vehicle to crawl past. But this figure evoked caution, causing me to move carefully along the chain-meshed fence. My first thought had been to dislocate: double back unseen and find another road that would slowly arch me back towards home. But I found a vague familiarity in his childish awkwardness and as he stepped under a convenient street lamp I realised where I had seen this man before.

Derrek had his dressing gown on but thankfully was still clothed beneath, a shirt and jumper that to date had prevented him from freezing, the top button done up - but he wore no tie. Looking down, I noticed he still wore his slippers over sockless feet. These were caked in thick soil which had crept up the hem of his trouser leg. He made no sign of recognition as I approached; lost in his crumbling thoughts, he did not seem to notice me at all. Even when I stood opposite him, reaching out to tug lightly on his hanging sleeve, he seemed content to ignore my intrusion, turning as though to walk away before his memory scrabbled again and he stopped as if to start his deliberations from scratch. As his mind fitfully turned, his lips quivered but no words fell from them; he blinked constantly as though trying to shake the mist from his brain.

"Mr Derrek?" I said, cringing at my inability to recall his full name.

Derrek did not seem to take offence, finally turning to look down on me, his brow creasing briefly from a total lack of recognition. It was at this moment I realised that this was the first time I had ever actually spoken to the man and had to accept that, even for those without Derrek's condition, I am not the most memorable of people. What limited statements and proximity that have occurred at the bus station, barely definable as conversations, have always been with his wife. Even those few words to enquire about this man were always relayed to him by his long-suffering proxy.

Derrek's dressing grown was old but made of thick fluffy fabric. I allowed my hand to slip down to take his fragile hand, feeling the brittle bones beneath the loose canopy of skin. Even when compared to my exposed fingers his small claw felt ice-like. He was also shaking and I noticed his jaw move beneath the hanging fleshless features like the mechanical chomp of a ventriloquist's dummy.

"Are you lost, Mr Derrek?" I asked. We were at least a mile from the bus stop and I had no idea where he lived. For once I found myself looking up and down the street in hope of company, but only the soft movement of the trees answered my call for assistance. Derrek did not answer my question, and pulled away slightly, turning once more as though set to shuffle away into the darkness. Yet, the light grip of his dressing gown was enough to arrest him. He remained content to be snared, left to look forlornly in his intended direction of travel. Yet he was happy to be guided, remaining pliable, allowing me to turn him to face me. Despite the cold there was only a vague lingering sense of alarm in his features.

I dislocated and slid my hands within the folds of fabric, his gown and trouser pockets, and felt down his ribs. I studied Derrek's face while my hands went to work, his frozen state somehow more expressive than his semi-animated self. There was a serenity to his gaze, a slight but noticeable improvement to his otherwise endless insecure self-doubt.

I was not even sure what I was looking for until my fingers detected the soft leather of his wallet. But this was no robbery. There was nothing to take anyway, the soft leather folder containing little other than a few low denomination coins, some long out of date documents and a single photo. But flipping over the wallet the clear plastic caught the light of the street light. The address was close, barely two hundred yards from the point Derrek has lost his bearings. A small polite notice in the shaking handwriting of his wife directed us back along Casewick Avenue.

If Derrek was surprised that I was miraculously suddenly holding his wallet he did not show it. He was thinking once more about leaving, using his superior weight to pull slowly away, dragging his slippers on the concrete to retreat in the opposite direction to that he had just previously intended.

Despite this, I was slowly able to coax him to turn around, to lead him by the cord of his dressing gown back in the direction of his home. The houses were small but well maintained, most were set back behind hedges and small trees. None had lights within them but many were still illuminated by porch light. Yet, a combination of darkness and the use of names instead of numbers made it difficult to find the right house. I worked under the assumption that neither of the old couple could drive so many of the houses were discounted. It was with the help of this deduction that I was finally able to find the property. Theirs was a small bungalow with wicker chairs on the lawn. Amongst the flower beds lurked the glass eyes of various cheap animal sculptures and an ugly birdbath formed out of crumbling cement. There was no car and the small painted wooden gate had been left open, presumably as Derrek had left it as he waddled past. I knew something was wrong when I got to the end of his front garden. There were no lights on in the house but the front door was open. Now on his doorstep, Derrek was more easily manoeuvrable. He took the lead, returning back into the gloom of the house. Despite this, I still lingered on the threshold and rang the bell, listening to the chimes echo through the still house. I also called out but to no effect.

Inside, I turned on the light and shut the door. The house was ordered, if cluttered. At the door I found a scarf and hat and I stopped to dress Derrek, closing the door behind him. He was shaking violently by now, a rattling chatter to his teeth, but was still enduring his ordeal in silence. Thankfully the house was warm and after squeezing past him in the corridor

I was able to press him up against a long radiator. The old woman had been washing her bed

linen and the sheets that were hung in the hall were now dry. These, too, I added to the layers

of Derrek's garments, casually throwing them over his head as though covering furniture with

a dustsheet. The effect was the same as a curtain being drawn over a parrot's cage. Derrek

seemingly took no offence or felt no humiliation at being covered in such a manner.

"Stay, Derrek, stay!"

I called out into the house again but my inquisitive 'hello' was met with more silence.

On the small table by the door I found some envelopes addressed to Mr and Mrs Parker. This

reminded me of the old woman and now, armed with a name, I was confident to explore

deeper into the house.

"Mrs Parker?" I called, pushing at the door to my right, feeling along the wall for the

light switch. The room was a continuation of the corridor, cluttered and not much bigger.

There was just enough room for a small table with two wooden chairs set at opposite ends,

and a squat glass cabinet filled with a mixed assortment of crockery. The table was set for

dinner but I suspected that it had not been used for some time. I doubt that there is much

point in seeking such structure for a meal where the old woman would only have her own

thoughts for company. The walls were covered in framed photographs and the mantelpiece

over the small fire was cluttered with various porcelain figurines and two small trophies.

Even coming in from outside I found the room was cold, and I didn't need to extend my hand

to realise that the radiator in this room had been turned off. There was also the smell of wood

polish, a clean and pleasant scent but overpowering in such an enclosed space. It was as

though, even in such a small house, this room has been allowed to slip into quiet and orderly

abandonment. I imagined it to be a relic to their previous lives and that I was the first person

to have stepped through this door for a number of years.

Though Mrs Parker remained unaccounted for, I found myself lingering, looking at the young smiling faces in the pictures, trying to match the youthful energy, enthusiasm and intelligence of the young man in the uniform to that shivering figure in the hall with the sheet cast over him. One photograph in particular held my attention. They were older now, Mrs Parker was dominating the picture as though to take an additional burden of their relationship. Derrek was smiling but he seemed smaller, less secure and lacking the focus to fully engage in the moment. The rot had started to set in, and you could see that both of them knew it. I imagined that the framing and hanging of this photograph was the last act of them, in this room as a meaningful living space: a high water mark. I imagined this moment being swollen with melancholy, neither of them turning back to take one final look at their life together before closing the door behind them for the final time.

My attention was broken by the soft patter of feet. The dog, Dorothy, sniffed suspiciously at my shoe before painfully raising a paw to scratch at my leg, reminding me of the purpose of my quest. I called out for Mrs Parker again but the growing weight in my gut told me that I would receive no answer. Back in the hall Derrek had pulled the sheet from his head. He had worked his way into the kitchen and I could hear the opening of drawers and the rattle of cutlery; though my attention was now focused on the other door. This one was slightly ajar and when I focused I could detect the faint crackle of a television set.

The door swung back quietly on its hinges to reveal a monochromatic scene. The white light from the television creating sharp shadows and contours, the gentle hum of the speakers providing a little energy. Compared to the two previous rooms, this space was Spartan, the two high-backed chairs and the small television dominating the room. The dog lurched slowly past where I stood and my eye line followed its movements. It completed a hobbling lap of the thick woollen rug before collapsing in front of the small gas fire.

This was the first dead person I had ever seen but the image did not seem unfamiliar to me. Mrs Parker sat watching television, a cup of tea still delicately balanced on the arm of her chair, a half finished magazine draped page down across her lap. She did not look at peace, just empty, like the statues of my dislocations. It was a parody so believable that I had to check that I was not in fact holding my breath.

Slowly, I reached out to touch her tepid flesh, expecting the tiny frame to simply crumble under the softest of caresses. My finger came to rest on the back of her delicate hand before pushing gently against her cheek. There was no resistance to the intrusion, the dry skin yielding without complaint, and as I withdrew my finger it took time for the unresponsive features to push back the small indentation I had created.

The pale light from the television only added to the vacuum of life and no light now reflected in the cataract eyes; her thin cracked lips were parted, the gap just sufficient for her last weak breath to have escaped. I found myself wondering how long she had been dead, trying to think about what fleeting thoughts may have passed through her mind in that instant. As though to gain perspective, I lowered myself into the empty armchair, mimicking her pose as though to simulate Mrs Parker's demise.

My study of the corpse was interrupted by the sound of a door slam - Derrek was on the move and as I turned his lumbering frame passed the door, the biscuit barrel tucked under his arm. At this the dog was also alert but yet to muster the energy to tear it away from the fire. I listened to the old man fumbling with the door handle but after only a moment he was back, loitering at the doorway before once more pacing with short dragging steps in the direction of the kitchen.

Even now I struggle to articulate my thought processes at that moment, my opinions on Mrs Parker remain vague and inconclusive. I guess part of me was sad, sorry that she was dead, sorry for whatever hurt or fear she may have felt in those final moments. As a show of

92

solidarity I took deep breaths and dislocated, but in this still space it did not seem to make any difference. If anything, Mrs Parker seemed more alive, finding momentary commonality with those she had recently left behind. But there was also another emotion: a selfish twinge of jealousy. Mrs Parker has escaped. She had fled this room, the dog, the graffiti-strewn bus stop and what remains of her husband. She had escaped me, and while I did not feel a loss for her absence, I did, in part, resent that she had not thought to take me with her.

As I breathed out, the only change was the return of the television's static and a slight twitch of the dog's stump-like tail. Watching television is strange while dislocated. You do not, as you might expect, get a flat, static picture. Rather, the image degrades, as though the colour bleeds like a stain through fabric. Here, of course, there was just white snow and the screen became an opaque grey mirror, an appropriate form of entertainment for the dead eyes of Mrs Parker. The glare also hurt my eyes to look at it, inducing a sharp localised ache at the very base of my neck, causing me to blink continually. I can offer no explanation as to why televisions have this effect. No other light source causes this. I can, if I wish, look at the sun during dislocations and it appears to me little more than a brilliant yellow marble. So, to avoid this pain, I cast my eyes around the room, turning my head across the ceiling like some bored child in church. Ultimately, my attention fell back on Mrs Parker and, by the association of her absence, the bleak future of her husband. I did not speak out loud, but in my head I spoke with Mrs Parker and I imagined that she in turn responded, offering impartial observations in keeping with our brief and functionary bus stop conversations. I imagined giving her some words of comfort, some guarantee as to the care of Derrek, but I was not sure she was either listening or cared. She was now either free or did not exist, and as far as I can determine, there is little to choose between these options.

The dog stretched its arthritic legs and set off in search of one of Derrek's biscuits, leaving Mrs Parker and I alone with our non-existences. Yet I did at least remember my commitment, finally offering the belated apology for my behaviour when we first met. Thankfully, I imagined that she accepted this token gesture with humility, modesty, and the grace of a woman who has borne so much throughout her long life. Good manners cost nothing when you are dead.

We chatted about a great number of things, discovering that there was much commonality between us. I found the conversation relaxed and non-judgemental, testament to Mrs Parker's current disposition which gave me more confidence than I would otherwise have been able to muster. I even found I was able to speak at length about my school and Dr Attwood's sessions. To both topics Mrs Parker offered some significant insight which reassuringly mirrored my own opinion. I took solace that she could still retain such empathy.

Eventually, the topic of Derrek came around, but to this she was somewhat dismissive. I suspect that it must have been a relief for her to have escaped him. Yet I had enjoyed Mrs Parker's company and wished to reciprocate her kindness. For a moment I even considered offering to look after Derrek in her absence, but we both knew that this was not going to be feasible and, in all likelihood, I did not expect that Mrs Parker would wish to see me struggle under this burden. Instead, I offered to take and look after Dorothy, and for this Mrs Parker was grateful. The dog had been a great source of comfort to her and, while willing to surrender Derrek's care to the authorities, her worries had in the recent days been increasingly focused on her scruffy friend.

As though to seal my pledge I once more reached over and lay my hand on Mrs Parker's. In this act the bruises around my wrist became visible and I imagined Mrs Parker catching a glimpse of them out of the corner of her dead eyes. I think she looked sad, a weary pity for the labours she knew I had suffered and would yet endure should I live to her advanced age. Finally all the concern, built from her observations at the bus stop, found utterance and Mrs Parker asked me how I got them. At first I considered lying, not for fear or embarrassment but from an unwillingness to burden this kind old lady with my own miseries. But she was earnest and accommodating and I did not think for one moment she would have believed me. I am not a good liar, and a poor lie would now have sullied our warming relationship.

She listened patiently and in silence as I told her about the girls gripping my wrists. I tried to give more details of the various beatings and humiliations, but they are by now so numerous that they meld together and I struggle to recall the precise details or times and places. But at that moment the countless repressed memories surged forward, fighting for disclosure, turning my careful and concise narrative into a gabbling and disjointed stream of consciousness. Yet Mrs Parker was patient and listened intently. Only when I began to lose my train of thought did she offer any form of encouragement, giving me the confidence to continue without fear of rebuke.

The process was cathartic and through those narratives it was as though Francis Kelly found some meaningful voice. The pain of the memories remained but it was somehow less traumatic, more manageable; the removal of the corrupting effects of the constant suppression rendering them less toxic to my person. What was until then a dirty catalogue of my own failings was now a list of grievances and unpunished offences against my person, validated by Mrs Parker as my confidante and witness.

"Why did you not dislocate?"

The question caught me off guard, momentarily unbalancing me and evoking my normal defensive suspicions. Yet now that Mrs Parker is dead I guess it is not surprising that she is familiar with the concept. I told her that this was mainly because I did not want to reveal my secret, but also because I have never really considered it. Mrs Parker's advice was equally as shocking and it made me feel uncomfortable. I am not a violent person.

The clumsy arrival of Derrek broke the conspiratorial mood. The sheet I had hurled over him was now draped around his shoulders like some ghoulish shroud. Yet he was still carrying the biscuit tin, now held out at arm's length as though it were some ceremonial object. Dorothy followed at his heels, craning her neck in hope of treats. I imagined I heard Mrs Parker's resigned sigh, a melancholic expression of loss, a regret as to the inevitable decay that all in the room had suffered. Yet despite this regret the room was warm and comfortable and it was a combination of this and the creeping fatigue which slowly gained ascendancy. I guess it was at this point that I fell asleep.

Flashes of blue light punctured the gaps in the curtains and I could hear the dog barking in the other room. The police officer had pushed Dorothy into the room of old memories and I think she now feared that it too was to be sealed in and abandoned. I didn't recall calling the ambulance, and as I looked around I was not even sure there was a telephone in the house.

"You frightened the crap out of me," the female officer said for the third time. She tried to appear angry but there was a hint of relief in her voice which undermined her authority. I guess it was just relief that they were only dealing with one body and not two. We had both jumped as I had woken, the officer emitting a piercing scream as my eyes flicked open.

After regaining their composure, I was quickly ushered out of the room and there was insufficient time to say much in the way of a goodbye to Mrs Parker. The television continued to rustle with static but the effects of its silver light now competed with other sources. The lights had been turned on throughout the house, stripping the room of intimacy and allowing reality to come crashing in with the officers. The scene of Mrs Parker's death now seemed cheap and ordinary.

Here, I waited as the paramedics went to work. I was asked no questions and no explanation for my presence was sought. Derrek was taken away and it was not until ten minutes later that the fat officer finally took ownership of me, his broad paddle-like hand laid heavily across the base of my neck as he steered me from the house and sat me down in his patrol car. The other officer had taken some liberties with Mrs Parker's kitchen and had made me a cup of sweet tea. I don't usually like tea, but I drank it gratefully and ate the accompanying biscuit. I do not imagine Mrs Parker would take offence.

My absence allowed the paramedics to wheel the trolley into the small house but the policeman was ready to take me home before Mrs Parker made her appearance. It was only when I reminded the police that they remembered the small dog and made no objection to Dorothy riding in the car as long as we sat on the back seat. The journey was a short one, but I liked being in the car and I dislocated numerous times to increase its longevity. The policeman said it was too early to put the lights and sirens on and he also ignored my request to be led up to the house in handcuffs.

XVI

"Do you feel angry, Francis?"

Yes I do, Dr Attwood, yes I do. Mine is a pathetic, wasteful and impotent rage and I sometimes fear I will simply be ripped apart by this directionless hate. My anger has passed the point where I can conceivably quantify or even name it and it is as though every waking moment and experience somehow adds to its critical mass. I believe that, were it not for the dislocation, I would already have lost all semblance of control, as though the rage would force its way straight out from my chest and mouth. At times, I have to dislocate just to keep my rage from crushing my sanity. The anger is still there; at such times it becomes localised and manageable, a silent emotional high frequency vibration, radiating malice like heat from hot coals. Only in such moments do I find the sensation both pleasant and empowering. Only now does the rage have focus and clarity.

I, of course, tell Dr Attwood none of this - there are degrees to which I am willing to reveal my instability. While my misfortunate nature will invariably produce the occasional undesired outburst which betrays and exposes me, I wish to keep these lapses to a minimum. This is, I assume, the desired result from my therapy, for Dr Attwood to reassemble poor old Francis to the point that she stops making a scene and embarrassing herself. This is certainly my parents' hope, but I am beginning to suspect Dr Attwood's interests may be a little more complicated.

I think that I am becoming increasingly valuable to her research and her career. I know she has written numerous books, many of which, I understand, have been well received in professional circles. In these volumes she discusses various patients in significant detail and on occasion I think that I can see her drafting a chapter of her next book in her head as she speaks to me. In fairness to her, I have found no hint of this in her notes; in fact, during some sessions, she rarely writes anything at all, a fact I find rather irritating. This has in turn led me to wonder whether Dr Attwood is recording our sessions. I do not know if this is ethical. I have dislocated many times to conduct a thorough search of the office but have not located either microphones or recording equipment. While I am generally ambivalent to Dr Attwood's poking and probing this would displease me. But this is mainly because I dislike the sound of my own voice. The vast majority of our sessions are little more than pregnant pauses as Dr Attwood waits for me to speak. My own voice, that flat and grating whine which I have had the displeasure to hear on answer machines and recordings, rarely features at all.

I did have a momentary flash of terror at the thought that my dislocations might produce some tell-tale sound. A jet plane produces some sonic boom as it passes the speed of sound and I wonder whether there is some corresponding popping or whooshing noise that accompanies my dislocations. If there is a sound, I imagine it as some sort of high-pitched squeak. But despite numerous tests I am confident that my detachments from time do not even produce a whisper. If equipment exists that can detect the collapsing vacuum of the spaces I leave behind I cannot tell you. Though if it does, I doubt Dr Attwood would have access to it.

I have spent much time trawling through her files during dislocations, but as I am limited to the capacity of a single breath, the process is time consuming and on the whole I have discovered little. I think most of the really interesting stuff is in her computer anyway. I have been able to find out some information about other patients but nothing specific about me. This was interesting only in so much as it made me realise just how many children are inherently damaged, some of them seemingly even more messed up than I. At times, away from Dr Attwood and her questions, I have thought about them and wondered whether they too can dislocate, considering whether their own unique cocktail of neurosis and maladjustments may have forced some equally unique and advantageous coping mechanisms.

In the final analysis, Dr Attwood can write whatever she likes. If whatever misunderstanding she derives from our stunted conversations can help her build some career then good luck to her.

The trouble is, I do take a little offence at her interest in my 'situation'. Sometimes, she does let the mask of professionalism slip, just a fraction, but enough to show me that she is enjoying her work. This seems unkind and I sometimes feel that it is the various anti-social aspects which she is fixating on and that, if she could, she would get rid of Francis Kelly entirely in order that she might be left in peace to study and dissect whatever aspect it is that is inherently corrupted or broken. She is in this capacity at least consistent with the prevailing opinion of my peers, but it sometimes feels a little awkward, like when you are getting in the way of a conversation, ruining the intimacy between the doctor and her specialism.

"How do you see yourself, Francis?"

I dislike how she puts my name at the end of every question. It is like I am taking part in some form of audition, being cast for some unspecified role. I find myself wondering about the other children who sit in this chair and I wonder whether they also get asked the same cyclic sequence of queries. I suspect I am merely the latest subject to be posed such questions, benchmarked against the response of the rest, charted somewhere in a bell shape curve. I suspect I am towards the extremities. I am simply one small component, a unit of data, in some larger study. Though I must admit that this thought does not unduly displease or distress me.

"How do you see yourself, Francis?"

If I was to answer the doctor's question with a degree of honesty, I would have to say that in the main I do not see myself at all. What self-awareness remains is seen from the perspective of my dislocations and my efforts to understand the parameters of my abilities. I learn that my dislocations are not total and I am still linked, though admittedly tentatively and with concessions, to the physical world. The most noticeable of relationships is with relation to light and gravity, as it seems that both functions somehow remain unaffected despite my fundamental manipulation of time. I find this a strange and unresolved arrangement as, with the cessation of time, I would expect the world to be plunged into immediate darkness, restricted to what limited light I can press against my retinas in my laboured movements through the stationary void. Yet my ability to perceive my environment remains unimpaired. The best theory I have come up with is that perhaps I have still fallen short of the ability to stop time in its entirety, merely having reduced it to such an extent that the remaining movement is so glacial that it occurs at a rate beyond my comprehension. Light, meanwhile, being so unfathomably fast as to negate any observable effect. Even in a second-rate school such as mine there are books which detail such issues. But the content is far beyond my comprehension.

Similarly unique is my continuing adherence to physical gravity. While my dislocation leaves the world in temporary stasis, an object like a drop of water, bird, or insect will hang suspended in animation. I have a personal relationship with gravity that remains, on the whole, unaltered. The relative dynamics between objects, their mass and the forces that they exert are, however, fundamentally perverted. While my dislocated world is static, it remains interactive and I soon learnt that my ability to influence this catatonic world is not limited to parting the gaseous soup to navigate. With these forces suspended, I find I can move objects of significant size as though mounted on invisible rollers; with pressure applied they slide across frictionless planes with ease and in whatever directions I push them. Large and ridiculously heavy objects can be raised within the parameters of my reach or rotated around the localised point of the centre of their mass. I can now redesign the world around

101

me, tinker with the fundamentals of existence and become the master of my environment. But it is an empty environment. Isolated in that instance, things lose their function and purpose: they become mere shapes, three-dimensional volumes. They become valueless and meaningless, devoid of aesthetic or emotional content. As do the people I observe. In this moment they possess no living energy or humanity. They are just crude statues, no different from a chair or a coffee cup; just another object, a shape, different from other shapes only in terms of their dimensions, colours and complexity.

I therefore find it hard to summon the enthusiasm to make fundamental changes to the world. Following lengthy introspection, I conclude this simply reaffirms my core belief that this is a world which I am no longer part of and have no real interest in. On the whole, I am content to remain the passive observer of each moment, navigating the limited range of my lung capacity, sampling the instant for what it is and leaving it as it is.

XVII

I'm being prescribed white pills at the moment. Last month they were blue and two months before that a sort of brownish grey. The name of the drug is long, it is hyphenated and has lots of 'x's' and 'y's' in it. I can't pronounce it but I have looked them up on the internet and found the reading pretty disconcerting. The side effects are numerous, some - like the loss of libido - are personally irrelevant but the nausea and potential loss of bladder control is not something I think anyone should take lightly. I notice how the marketing literature uses the word 'potentially' liberally throughout the text. It is as if, were any of the many documented side effects to occur, I should be in some way surprised to be so unlucky. This word is also noticeably absent when describing the therapeutic effect. To my mind, this is a significant oversight considering that none of the previous medicines prescribed for me achieved anything tangible. You also have to wonder why this particular drug is so far down the pecking order in Dr Attwood's repertoire if such miraculous transformations are truly possible in easy to swallow capsules.

This is not the first time I have been prescribed some new miracle drug. Many combinations have been tried and I will continue to skew their carefully manicured research data by not taking them. This is not just obstinacy on my part. The previous me, the pre-dislocated Francis Kelly, put great faith in her parents, her doctors, and her psychologists and their various snake oils. She took them at their word and swallowed the tablets for prolonged periods. She took them, fully conceding the fact that the good ship Francis is rudderless and listing badly. I vaguely recall periods of optimism, not through any tangible benefit of the drugs but built purely on the basis that such success might be possible. I bought into the potential that Francis Kelly, through two tablets a day, taken with food, might eventually be reborn. I imagined her waking one morning to be embraced by society, the prodigal daughter having returned from the wilderness of her disjointed isolation.

But even for someone as inherently ill-disposed to the world and their own body as I, the effects were far from pleasant. The worst medicine I have been prescribed being a short course of blue translucent circular pills, the effect being so disorientating, so numbing and exhausting that the eventual escape back to my disparate non-existence did genuinely feel like some new and meaningful advancement.

Since then, my ability to dislocate has enabled me to escape Dr Attwood's efforts to poison me. But I must be careful. I know my parents suspect I do not take my tablets and Dr Attwood questions me suspiciously about the lack of any apparent effects. Therefore, sleight of hand or hiding them under my tongue is not an option and I must dislocate with significant control to convince distrustful eyes that I have swallowed them.

In short, I have come to distrust claims of chemical salvation and the quackery of pharmaceuticals. I do not hold any sense of grievance against my parents, or even Dr Attwood for that matter. But to me it is clear that little has changed since the days of bone-rattling witch doctors. It is just that the leeches are now sugar coated and the equivalent of the hemlock incense comes in pink sachets of dissolvable powder. The effects are equally misunderstood. As far as I can see, those rare incidents of success are similar to slapping the side of an old television to get it to work properly. Yet I guess I should be grateful, I am under no illusions that, had I not been born in these 'enlightened' times, we would be only a few short steps to electro-convulsive therapy or lobotomy. Had I been born centuries earlier my persecutors would have by now had me burnt as a witch.

They will, regrettably, still keep experimenting with the latest mishmash of compounds, and I suspect that with each new licence Dr Attwood will be first in the queue in hope of a career-defining breakthrough. But what annoys me the most is that these current drugs are supposedly primarily for individuals suffering from paranoia.

I can state categorically that I am not a paranoid person and apart from one or two uncertain moments I can be pretty confident that I have never harboured such thoughts. Were Dr Attwood to genuinely seek my opinion of my condition, I would say that I am pretty far from such a state. I am under no delusion that the ubiquitous 'they' might be out to get me. I hear no voices whispering in my ears hinting at this, that, or the other. I am confident that aliens are not reading my thoughts, that I form no part in government conspiracies or that my food or water is being poisoned. I am so incensed by the association that I am even considering raising my objection with Dr Attwood. Possibly, for once, we might even have an open and frank discussion on the matter. This is a blatant misdiagnosis. Perhaps this is the point. Perhaps she is just prescribing me these pills to see if I am paying attention. The point I would seek to make is that a paranoid state is fundamentally reliant on a misguided belief of the importance of the individual who suffers the delusions. A paranoid person requires a heightened belief in themselves, a conviction that they are in some way of interest to shadowy agent provocateurs, or that people speak about them behind their backs and plot against them. I, however, am resigned to the fact that the world does not consider me a worthy project. I suspect that certain individuals do talk about me in derogatory terms but this is far from me being paranoid. In my case they are out to get me, actively and with significant intensity. I have the injuries to prove it.

Yet I harbour no illusions, no visions of grandeur as to my relative importance or interest. If there is a diametrically opposite condition to being paranoid then perhaps this is a more meaningful starting point for any medical intervention.

XVIII

"Kelly!"

My dislocations do not protect me when I turn to the call of my name and receive a crippling blow to the stomach, the guttural shock of a hockey stick swung violently into my abdomen. In an instant I am bent forward on my knees as my brain and body revolts, a shuddering desire to vomit compounded by a flickering strobe effect on time itself as my laboured breaths repeatedly bring me to the cusp of dislocation. It is a twisting pain, the sound of my lungs wheezing, groping for air, and the fading laughter of my receding classmates. Despite my pain, the unavoidable truth is quite clear. This is a lesson which, at its heart, is a less than gentle reminder that I am tethered to a body that craves for air, for food and water, and that stepping into the still and stable world of my dislocation is at best a fleeting moment of escape.

XIX

"I would like, if I could, to talk about what is worrying you. I'd like you to be able to tell me what you are scared of."

As a matter of course, at the end of each session I dislocate to read whatever the doctor thinks she has observed. From my intelligence gathering I know that the doctor suspects that my fears are numerous and varied, that they are derived from a deep-rooted lack of self-worth and the subsequent loneliness that comes from my inability to form relationships with those my own age. Yet, these notes no longer accurately reflect my current anxieties. My dislocated sense of fear is as inert as the stationary world that surrounds me and I have shaken free of my fears through my numerous personal exclusions from the fabric of reality.

I hide from my classmates in order to avoid their assaults but I question whether this constitutes a genuine fear. The pain and humiliation is thoroughly unpleasant but having now demoted, if not outright rejected, the concept of 'Francis Kelly' I am increasingly uncaring as to her trials and outrageous fortunes. Perhaps if Francis were more interesting, or not so incapable of the most rudimentary processes, I might reassess my opinion of her. But as far as I can see she does not really seem worth the effort. In this respect I am amazed that others still take the time and effort to repeatedly injure her.

Yet there is one significant fear I cannot share with the doctor, which now fills the void left by the others. My inability to prevent the impact of my dislocation when I hold my breath has given birth to one significant danger which is now manifesting itself into a growing and overwhelming phobia.

The realisation of this new fear occurred to me as I washed myself, plunging my head into clear, cool water and instantaneously finding my head immersed in the thick granular mass that encased and confined my face. It now seems such an obvious oversight but at the time I can assure you it was quite a shocking discovery. There was more than a hint of panic in that moment, where I struggled to pull my face from the basin, my ears rubbed painfully forward as the water dragged across my skull. The collapse of the indentation as I exhaled caused a grey wave of soapy water to cascade onto the bathroom floor.

At that moment, the grave implications of my discovery were eclipsed by this new wonder and I dunked my head back into the basin, dislocating, to repeat the novel experience. Once free, I stared at the vacuum I had created, a watery death mask, staring back at me from the basin. Maintaining the dislocation, I now remember how I struggled to pass my hand through this resistant substance, trying, and failing, to find suitable descriptions for this alien texture.

With a naïve childish glee I recall running a shallow bath, my patience only allowing a few inches of depth to rise before gingerly stepping onto the smooth surface, to stand perched above the clear, solidified liquid. For an instant, my mind revolted, struggling to accept the world without gravity. It was not until some days later that the threat that this medium presents dawned on me.

It was my forever eager peers who became my unlikely teachers. Their hunting party arrested me on the canal side; the pushing and slapping proving unsatisfactory entertainment soon gave way to the genesis of their plan, evolving into the idea of hurling me into the sludge-like water. Ironically, for once, there was no meaningful violence, but with the threat came the realisation and with the realisation soon came an all-encompassing horror.

I do not know whether it was their half-hearted ambivalence that enabled me to escape or that my terrified thrashing had reached a hitherto unseen frenzy. At that point, at least, I deeply cared for Francis Kelly, striking blindly with flailing limbs, losing shoes and scratching with bloody fingernails to claw my way inch by inch from the precipice. At points I even dislocated, enough to seize the initiative, my screams reaching such a crescendo that I suspect that my terror became infectious, saturating my attackers. The effect more devastating than my ill-timed and ineffective blows.

By the time they retreated, leaving me sobbing, sweating but otherwise dry, my fear was already so far ingrained as to rarely leave my waking thoughts. At first, I clung to the misguided belief that I might somehow be exempt, but a rudimentary experiment submerged in my parents' narrow bathtub was sufficient to dispel such hopes.

Alongside the suspension of gravity, there is also a suspension of the Archimedean forces that could levitate me to safety. Even in my carefully controlled experiment I underestimated the threat and obtuse nature of dislocated water. I had barely submerged myself an inch below the surface before the dislocation took its devastating effect. It was as though I was encased in concrete. Had I not had the foresight to keep both my arms raised, I fear I would never have pulled myself free. The force was smothering, all-encompassing, and even with such little liquid above me I found myself unable to raise myself. With increasing desperation, my white knuckles gripped the edge of the bath, pulling with all my feeble strength to haul myself clear. Finally, reaching the point of exhaustion, the idea that saved my life flashed across my panicked mind. Releasing my grip of the bathtub, I began to claw at the thick paste, scraping it away from my nose and mouth, forming thick banks, buying enough time for me to steal a quick breath before the walls of water came crashing down.

So now I am gripped with the acute fear that I will find myself submerged, dislocating, unable to either reach out of the constricting liquid or touch the bottom with my feet, capable only of making minor indentations on the suffocating glue, like a child making angel shapes in snow. Even to someone as passive to their own wellbeing as I, it seems such a horrific and lonely death. A death made worse by the foretelling.

I would simply be held entombed; unable to exhale or breathe, suffocating with the only chance of rescue being to wilfully force myself to allow the water to cascade into my lungs in the hope that time might reassert itself, and that someone nearby might rescue me. I fear my own weakness as I know, if faced with such a nightmare scenario, I would not have the strength of mind to accept that this would be my only chance of salvation.

But, despite this, I still enjoy the rain when dislocated. I like watching its resinous globules solidify like tar, feeling the glass-like absence of moisture, the sensation of moving through the speckled and pitted environment as though navigating through a haze of marbled insects. I derive a strange delight when plucking a droplet of water from my skin like some crystal beetle and, rather than feeling it dissolve and escape, roll it between my fingers as it holds belligerently firm to its form.

XX

This isn't easy, you know. It is difficult to give anything close to a complete and balanced description when you have no alternative perspective or opinion. Just try it yourself and you'll quickly see what I mean. Go on, try. Try and explain what it is like to be normal. It's tough, isn't it? Very hard to be precise, very difficult to clearly articulate just what it is about you that is suitably similar to everyone else to the point at which it becomes something you don't have to unduly worry yourself about. Perhaps that is it, perhaps this is what does give me a small technical advantage. For as long as I can remember I have been made acutely aware that there are many aspects of 'me' that I should be increasingly concerned about. It gives a certain perspective.

XXI

I have a nemesis. I imagine this sounds a little exaggerated but I really can think of no other way to describe her. The word conjures images of superheroes and villains, blood-soaked vendettas and terrible revenges for heinous crimes. Sadly, I suspect the truth is far more mundane. But the exact cause for the endless attrition remains a mystery to me.

Perhaps it is unfair for me to single this one girl out. It is true that she is not my sole persecutor, and my unpopularity in school has now reached the point where my systematic victimisation is almost a prerequisite to normal, everyday interaction between my classmates. However, even those small and random acts of unkindness from the extended support cast of my antagonists seem to be built on the firm foundation of my nemesis's inherent dislike for my person. It is as though she has normalised the abuse, and when not actively orchestrating the humiliation she is serving as a catalyst to those who are.

Her name is Rebecca Shiels. She is a girl in my year and a number of my classes, but that is about as far as the similarity goes. I guess you could say she is a girl of average proportions, and this of course means she is both taller and bigger than I. We are comparably thin I guess, but while her figure portrays a healthy, slim athleticism, mine is associated with a dishevelled emaciation. I guess others might say she is pretty but I am no great judge of beauty and I find little pleasing in her appearance. I am also not the best person to give an opinion as to whether she is a popular girl, but she is obviously held in better regard than me.

I have heard it said that bullies are just cowards, and if you stand up to them they will invariably back down. This is, I can reliably inform, utter rubbish. They may very well be cowards. But cowards know they are cowards and as such rely on animalistic cunning. Key to this is ensuring that no opportunity for their own humiliation presents itself. Those who exercise such tendencies are also not without their own abilities. They are great orchestrators of mobs, and naturally attune to identifying weaknesses in others and channelling the insecurities of their peers. They create theatre, becoming actors, playing to the crowd, inviting them into a carnival of their own design.

Rebecca Shiels is excellent in this capacity. Through her verbal skills she is formidable, a natural orator, armed with hundreds of cheap and childish slights at my expense. She is relentless with these little digs and comments, all aimed to degrade and entertain in equal measure. But it is her skilful manipulation of those around her that is most effective. She now rarely strikes me herself, rather it is her less cerebral minions who do this grunt work. As I have already said, the boys at my school ignore me, though this girl is not opposed to the occasional enlistment of their muscle through manipulation of their puppyish desires. Usually their presence is beneficial, with Rebecca's attention focused on her own prestige and her charade of feminine charms. These appear embarrassingly clumsy to me, yet are seemingly used to great effect in the eyes of her peers. In such instances, I am no form of threat to her and have on occasion even been the recipient of some small token of her magnanimity.

It has now reached the point where it is as though Rebecca has outsourced the tedious responsibility of my abuse, her toadying friends lining up to take over the mantle as though this represents some form of promotion. A squat and repellent girl by the name of Alison Townsend is proving herself particularly enthusiastic in this regard. She is a sort of ugly sidekick to Rebecca, her absence of wit and charm matched only by her catastrophic lack of self-confidence. All of which are traits Rebecca apparently values in her friend, her sullen company tolerated due to the need for a sycophantic, ego-massaging audience. Even I have to admit that Rebecca cannot help but appear enhanced when in close proximity to this girl.

Yet she certainly seems enthusiastic to bring a degree of physicality to Rebecca's caustic wit and slanderous insults. This is a more obvious manifestation of her ugliness and I genuinely get the sense that the violence is a response to her own deep-rooted frustration and unhappiness. In my next session, I might ask Dr Attwood for her business card. A few sessions of therapy for Alison Townsend might prove mutually beneficial. Therapy by proxy, if you like.

There are others; my reputation sufficiently advertised to seemingly enable anyone in the school to take liberties, an opportunity for my fellow students to work out their frustrations or bolster some flagging self-esteem. The school is a cocktail of insecurity and neuroses, and it is a testament to the extreme nature of my own condition that I do not feel totally at home. For some, the damage is so ingrained and obvious that I almost feel like I am providing some integral community service.

Not that my current school is much worse than its predecessors, the bitterness and confusion is simply distilling into an increasingly putrid malaise with the passing of each academic year. This is only the continual erosion of suffocating experiences, the increasingly brutal and desperate struggle for identity. Perhaps it is just that I have been at this school for longer than the previous ones, the final years of my education a little more informative and desperate. Perhaps it is only this which has offered me the opportunity to observe the corrupting effect of the toxic blend of institutions and feral immaturity. All of which lends a sense of indifference to the violence. To be alien, to not to belong or be accepted by this seething mass, feels more like a vindication than a punishment.

Yet I still crave some insight as to why I am being subjected to such scrutiny. Despite us all being test subjects of the horrendous nature of our environment, it must be noted that the vast majority of my classmates do, on the whole, drudge through their day either oblivious or indifferent to me. At times, I have imagined that Rebecca is serving some obscure but necessary function of the school's mechanism, enabling the rest of my classmates to go freely about whatever business is their own specific calling. I imagine that, were she not

114

there, were she somehow indisposed or incapacitated, it would fall on another child, most likely the forever-eager Alison Townsend, to step into the breech. I imagine that, were Alison also absent, this would result in some crippling damage to the smooth running of the school, the vacancy proving so problematic that it becomes necessary for a request to be made in morning assembly with Mrs Jenkins reading out the notice to the whole school, in search of willing volunteers. A temporary replacement would simply have to be found. And so the delegation would continue, on and on, each child having their place; a neat and seamless rank structure at which I am quite firmly rooted to the bottom.

Therefore, if it was not Rebecca, I guess, as with my previous schools, another child would have taken her role. I don't recall any particular event which would serve to have pointed me out to Rebecca. I can't even remember the first time we met, and certainly do not remember any conversations prior to the slow escalation of taunts, insults and vitriolic gibes.

Neither do I even remember the first time she hit or was cruel to me. It was as though we had both slid seamlessly into our roles, finding each other compatible, becoming co-dependent in this endless cycle of escalating violence. Maybe what transpires between Rebecca and I is a lot like what took place between my teeth and Dr Bennett's forearm. There is a degree of irresistible inevitability about it. She is compelled, seemingly with no understanding or concept or potential of an alternative course of action, to victimise me whenever practically possible. She has simply submitted to the role as my persecutor, my nemesis, my enemy. I do hate her, but I should probably hate her more than I do. But maintaining and understanding my emotions and their causality has never been one of my strong suits and I am, I still believe, not inherently a violent person.

That said, I must acknowledge that this cycle of violence has turned in on itself. It has become a spiral, growing sharper and more twisted with every given day. As such, I feel the inevitability of this chain of events. I do not need to dislocate to anticipate the ultimate destination of this natural progression. We approach a threshold, the end of an epoch. What lies beyond this remains unclear but, from what has happened already, what has built us to this point, the accumulative effect will bring us to some final, potentially catastrophic, conclusion.

.

XXII

Pictures are curious things. The most alarming but overlooked aspect of them being that, for some reason, people think they are real. At the corner of the street opposite the school there is a small shop and above this is a billboard of significant proportions. A woman is smiling, her face measuring in the region of two metres in diameter. We are led to believe that this smile, this calm and expressive confidence, and her perfect airbrushed skin, is the result of the effects of a simple product. In this instance it is a yoghurt, but as far as I can tell the range of objects which contain the elixir to induce this ecstatic, life-affirming afterglow is almost limitless. Apparently, this sort of thing does my classmates and me untold damage, damaging our sense of self, leading to numerous anxieties, mental health problems, and eating disorders. They remind people that they are unhappy.

Dr Attwood thinks I have also been damaged in such a way, as various aspects of my condition mirror exactly the negative impacts of such a predatory and image-driven society. She has alluded to the possibility that it is my failure to comply, my failure to derive such emotional completeness and physical beauty through the endless consumption of yoghurts which is at the core of my condition. She asks me to think about myself. This is in itself a depressing experience, though on the whole I do not discriminate against Francis Kelly nor resent her for failing to approximate any of the numerous images plastered across the billboard. I do, however, pity such children if they exist, for their condition seems to parallel my own. I would even go so far as to say that there may be some commonality between us, at least in terms of symptoms. My lack of self-worth and my eating disorders are well documented, and the consumption of food is still little more than a mechanical replenishment of chemicals and a necessity for the prescription of my medication.

Apparently, this image is particularly damaging because it is 'aimed at me'. Other adverts, adverts for cars, beers, and sports equipment, do less damage to me because they are aimed at other people. Someone, somewhere, has taken the time to work out what I like. They have decided I need this yoghurt, and in their decision they have sown the seeds of my misery. This is because, while I pay for a yoghurt this is not what I am buying. I am buying a large two-dimensional smiling head. I am becoming a billboard above a corner of a shop at the end of a street. This, of course, makes no sense at all.

"Would you like to be like this woman, Francis?"

Coincidentally, in one of our sessions, Dr Attwood held up a page from her magazine to show the same smiling face as that of the billboard. Though this one measures only a few inches across. By way of an answer I just shrugged with indifference. I told Dr Attwood that I was under no illusion that Francis Kelly would ever be asked to sell yoghurt and I could imagine no quicker way for a company to go bankrupt than to enlist her as the posterchild of this, or any, product. Dr Attwood said that this is not what she meant, she said she wondered whether there were attributes of this woman that I desired, aspects of this woman I would gladly exchange my own for. I told Dr Attwood that she was holding up a picture, just a smiling head and a few manicured fingers. I told her that both were made out of paper. The doctor seemed unsatisfied with this response.

The yoghurt-wielding two-dimensional giant is also telling me to live in the moment. This is a phrase I hear regularly in the mantra of adverts and lifestyle gurus. My classmates like to paraphrase it in search of demonstration of spontaneity. People imagine 'the moment' as some snapshot of purity; the adverts and edited imagery portray the moment through the rose tinted glasses of reminiscence and nostalgia. They imagine it as the point at which the white noise of the world is dispelled, the place in which the heartfelt consideration of the meaning of your existence is achieved. In this mythical place, in this 'moment', the daydreamer finds a point in which the greatness of humanity and the smorgasbord of life's opportunity are laid out before them. This is a point at which they, now presented as some liberated third party observer, can sample and savour those fleeting thoughts, those hopes and fears, the loves and ambitions which are so frequently drowned under the tsunami of petty insecurities, insignificancies and daily chores. Even Dr Attwood succumbs to this fantasy and she has repeatedly promoted a need for mindfulness, urging me to give Francis Kelly more consideration, to consider her wretched existence, to ground it in the moribund and depressing formality of its immediate environment.

To live in the moment is a curse; the yoghurt-selling woman is promising damnation for all who aspire to achieve her wretched enlightenment. This is at best, at its most superficial level, just some lazy and meaningless soundbite. I have seen the moment. I have dislocated to the point where I have been able to study 'the moment' in all its ugliness. The moment is cold and inanimate, the moment is void of meaning and stagnated to the point of irrelevance. This is not a snapshot of life, this is not the moment to absorb the full panorama of existence. 'The moment' is a prison sentence, it is a cell. Once distilled through dislocation, I find nothing in these empty vessels. This is my epiphany, the knowledge that there is nothing in 'the moment', nothing in the moment that follows it, and nothing in any that subsequently come after that. Life is a crude cartoon stick man, doodled in the bottom corner of the Gods' notebooks. It is only as the deities' thumbs are drawn across these series of doodles, fanned to intimate movement, that the illusion of meaning is created. At any given instant there is simply nothing but the complex and contorted arrangement of atoms. This is the true nature of 'living in the moment', and I want nothing to do with it.

XXIII

Dorothy has become somewhat of a bone of contention within our already disunited household. Her immediate arrival escaped attention, my parents' sleep-deprived concerns firmly focused on the two police officers who calmly related details of Mrs Parker's demise while nursing mugs of flavourless instant coffee. The officers even gave a glowing account of my behaviour, confusing my already bewildered parents, causing them to not question the decrepit animal sniffing at their ankles. It was only in the morning, prompted by the sound of Dorothy scratching at my bedroom door for her morning ablutions, that my parents questioned me as to our new house guest.

It is safe to say that my parents' attitude to Dorothy is poor and unwelcoming. Though in truth the animal is far from the ideal pet. As her new carers, we must now tolerate the ravages of old age. The dog is mildly incontinent for a start, leading to heated discussions as to whether it should live in the garden. This was an opinion overruled by the fact that we all agreed it would be unlikely to survive the night. So she sleeps in my room, the unsanitary nature of my dwelling already sufficiently decayed to not significantly affect the rest of the house. Despite this, she has brought with her a certain odour, a mustiness which, while you habituate to it in her company, you are reminded of whenever entering the house. Along with the smell are the strange sounds. Even when resting, Dorothy wheezes, emitting a faint rasping sound similar to a heavy smoker or some enfeebled asthmatic. When she is asleep this is little better, her endless fight for breath mutating into a slow but resonating snore. Personally, I find something quite soothing about the gentle rhythm, but from time to time she stops mid-snore, the room becomes silent and we find all eyes turn to the dog. My concentration and train of thought at that moment is broken and I am unable to continue whatever it is I was doing until the animal either exhales or is confirmed as dead.

In addition to this, the animal moults excessively and I think my father may be allergic. Even with it expressly forbidden from being on the furniture and limited to only a few rooms in the house, the wiry little hairs seems to get everywhere and multiply at an alarming rate. The drone of our vacuum cleaner is now a continuous anthem and I would not be surprised to find the dog has become completely bald within a fortnight.

All of which leads us to accept the fact that Dorothy is not long for this world, and my father has muttered his fears of the spectre of ever-mounting vets' bills on more than one occasion. He was even at the threshold of raising the potential benefits of euthanasia before being browbeaten by my mother. I do have sympathy for his point of view, and I would not wish to see Dorothy suffer. But Mrs Parker would be unhappy and I gave her my word. We are not at that point just yet.

I retain an aloof fondness for Dorothy, though I would be lying to say she does not on occasion evoke my creeping irritation. Cleaning up after her is not a problem but I find the walks frustrating as she has in part curtailed the range of my various nocturnal wanderings around my neighbourhood. Dorothy simply can't walk any meaningful distance. It is as though her legs are now just short bristle-covered stilts and can, at best, totter a few yards beyond the limit of our front garden before seemingly losing all interest or memory of the intended journey we had embarked on. How Mrs Parker consistently navigated this animal to the bus station and beyond I have no idea. But I guess the same could be said of Derrek.

This at least is one aspect of Dorothy's presence which is pleasing to my parents: she has become some sort of furry manacle, enabling my mother to merely peer from between the living room curtains to locate her previous absent and roaming daughter. I think this is one of the reasons that my mother has become Dorothy's unexpected champion. Generally, she has a propensity to be scared of dogs, and will cross streets to avoid them even if they are on leads. However, even she can control her phobias when confronted with Dorothy's crippled remains. And I think she has great hope for the tender shoots of social interaction that this dog brings out of me.

I speak to Dorothy, mostly irritated pleas for her to hurry up - but this still constitutes more than I willingly say to either my parents or my classmates. I discount my dialogue with Dr Attwood here, as these are in the main simply responses to commands. Dorothy's inability to emit anything other than a whine, snort, or inopportune blast of flatulence is also conducive to the conversation. I recognise this poor animal as a mere prop for my rambling thoughts but it is good to air them beyond the confines of my own brain. At times such as this I am usually out of earshot. Those few random souls, my neighbours, who I pass in the darkness, are usually either sufficiently aware of my unstable nature to give me a wide berth or naturally ill-disposed to a young girl who mutters and argues with herself. The threat of mental illness, its spontaneity and unpredictability, is truly remarkable. I am, after all, hardly a significant physical specimen. Were I somehow to launch an attack I have no doubt that all but the most enfeebled would disable me with ease. Those few people to whom I could constitute a reasonable threat tend not to be found wandering the streets in the early hours.

Considering the time of year it does not seem that cold but the clear sky promises a swift drop in temperature and some of my neighbours have gone so far as to lay down grit and hurl blankets over windscreens in the hope of a swift start the following morning. Little life is detectable through the closed curtains of darkened houses. Only a few of my immediate neighbours have any lights on at all, those being bedroom lights. The stars provide some additional light but it appears we have lost the moon. A careless oversight by all accounts.

Dorothy has taken a liking to my neighbour's flower beds. At this time of year they are just short blackened stumps of shrubs, but even now they are keeping her interest. Considering her decrepit state she seems remarkably strong. This, though, is probably more a reflection of my own weakness and the need to show a high degree of restraint. I could easily yank the animal back onto the path but I fear that such force around so scrawny a neck would have dire consequences. She sniffs and paws at the ground before she finally, and painfully, lowers her shaking hind legs to squat over the frost-bitten remains of some plant. I sympathise with the plant for the indignity.

"Fwark, frwark, fwark!"

I am in the process of giving Dorothy my account of an insect I have been confusing recently when I hear it. At this time of year any call of a bird is strange but this call sounds particularly out of place. There is a mocking stupidity to it and I try to train my eyes to the darkness to see where the sound is coming from. My attention is drawn to a number of trees to my right. Though the foliage is all gone it still takes me time to identify shapes due to various thick branches casting shadows which move in the light breeze.

"Fwark, frwark, fwark!"

The headlights of a car turning into the road sweep across the lawns and parked vehicles. It momentarily blinds me but then conveniently pinpoints my quarry. Though very high in the tree, the object is much bigger than a bird. At first, the shape is vague and nondescript but as it moves it reveals itself to be the shape of a small boy. I am under no illusion as to who.

I tug on Dorothy's chain with irritation and begin to drag it back to the house before the third grating call pricks my curiosity. Having now identified the shape I can see him relatively clearly. He is waving, his enthusiasm causing the branches he is holding onto to sway violently from side to side. Foolishly, I find myself waving back, an act which irritates me even further. At first I think he has fallen but quickly realise it is just the speed at which he moves from branch to branch. The boy descends both quickly and precisely, at times he hardly grasps for the branches, merely leaning against them until his sure-footed hops find some purchase, using their natural elasticity to oscillate down to the lowest branches. By the time I get to the foot of the tree Billy is hanging upside down by his knees like some bat. He is grinning widely.

"What do you want?"

"Fwark! Fwark! Fwark!"

I can't help but smile. The boy is imbecilic, swinging like some deformed little monkey. But his diminutive figure hides significant aerobic strength and with a whip-like arch of his back he has swung, chimp-like, back into the branches.

"You coming up? View's great."

"It's pitch black."

"Not from the top it ain't."

A fear grips me. There is a small knot in the wood I can feasibly use as a hand grip but beyond that there is just the narrow grains of the bark and a fist-sized stump of aborted branches. All of which represents an opportunity for a fresh demonstration of my pitiful upper body strength.

Yet for some reason I am outraged at the thought of being beaten by this idiot, and after tying Dorothy to the base of a hedge I find myself exploring the side of the tree in search of a suitable place to take my grip. But despite this careful planning, after only raising myself at best a few feet above the ground, gravity refuses to be denied and I am unceremoniously dragged back to earth.

"I, I can't."

Billy is inverted again, offering out a hand. I don't want to touch it but no suitable alternative presents itself. At first, it is just a soft sweating palm, but as his fingers curl around my wrist an incredible power exerts itself, hauling me with sufficient strength to enable me to scramble up for more meaningful hand grips, keeping me airborne long enough for my flailing feet to find purchase. His other hand now grabs at the back of my coat and at any other time I would scream and convulse with such proximity. But now, those few feet seem like a deadly distance to fall and I cling as much to his arm as to the tree. It is this reluctance that means it takes time to heave my exhausted frame into the underbelly of the twisting lattice of branches.

With another inane grin Billy climbs effortlessly and without fear. But to me the drop already climbed now seems fatal, sure to crush my skull or snap both my ankles. Dislocations cannot help me now, my personal relationship with gravity remaining unaffected. Reality now gets ready to slap me in the face. Yet, against my better judgement, I tentatively continue to reach up for further branches, catching my clothes and scratching myself in sudden, jerking grasps. Thankfully, after about two more yards' climb Billy either loses patience or feels pity, dropping from the highest branches to perch like some feral cat on a sturdy branch. I try to look calm, an attempt I am confident I fail in achieving.

"You nervous?"

My initial reaction is to vomit all over him but I find some previously hidden resolve and restrain myself. Though he does not seem to be mocking me. His comment is some nervous attempt at observation. Billy Rowley is not a boy used to being right about things. Even the blindingly obvious. I shake my head.

"My mother has been to the chemist. The chemist says that when I get really excited I should take one of my tablets. My mother says being scared is a lot like being excited. Like a smile and an unhappy face are the same just the other way around."

Billy is rummaging in his jacket and finally pulls out a small plastic container which he shakes enthusiastically. From the sound I can determine that it is nearly empty. He struggles with the lid, which yields with a pronounced popping sound, and peers into the darkened mouth of the container like he is looking into some small telescope. Finally, his soft hand reaches down to drop two sizable chalk textured capsules into my palm. They are bigger than anything Dr Attwood has ever prescribed for me and it is too dark to see the label - and I don't recognise the bottle.

"They let you self-medicate?"

"Eh?"

"Your tablets, they just give you the whole bottle?"

Billy does not answer, but despite the darkness he throws one of the tablets to the back of his throat. I am pretty sure he has swallowed it before he has even had time to close his mouth.

A silence follows, awkward and unpleasant; the same relaxed smile seeks to reassure but there is something overbearing about it. I am not used to people giving me their full attention. It is not like the silence I evoke in Dr Attwood's office. This is pressing and claustrophobic, creating a vacuum which I feel I need to fill. But the sentence that starts to form in my mouth is not right and I don't like it. It is turning into an apology, to say sorry for shouting at him for ruining my colouring. I am momentarily outraged at myself and, were I not trapped in this tree, I would struggle to choke down my indignation.

"You get grief off Grimshaw?" I offer finally. Billy smirks and snorts a laugh.

"Nah, as soon as you vommed over the desk he forgot what we were talking about. Even let us go five minutes early so he could get the cleaners in before the afternoon lessons."

"Why did you come to my house?"

Here Billy just shrugs, but there is no embarrassment or blush in the darkness. It is a simple expression of ignorance, as though to walk half way across town was just a momentary impulse. For a moment he becomes absent minded, picking small twigs from the branch, swinging his legs to kick at the trunk of the tree with his heel.

"Dunno. I guess I just thought I'd say hi."

126

There is a pause, but thankfully it is Billy who keeps talking. It is a deviation from my line of questioning: telling me about himself, the name of the street his house is on and about his father's car. I don't recognise the street name and I don't know anything about cars. There is something strange about the account. It seems rehearsed, not memorised like a fabricated event but as though he is telling me what he watched on television and is now trying to remember the sequence of events so as not to ruin the story. He keeps referring to his father's car, randomly injecting it into the narrative as though this vehicle is some sort of sibling. He speaks openly but I do not reciprocate. The car is painted dugong. I tell him I don't know what that is and he says it is a lot like the cream colour of mushrooms.

"I've seen you at school, you seem sad."

It takes a while for me to realise that he has finally answered my question. It is as though everything that preceded it was just to build up to this simple statement. He had spoken for so long I had had time to prepare another question, to ask him why he climbed on top of the Portakabins. But below my feet Dorothy starts barking and I tell Billy I have to go. Billy says he should be going home as well but I don't believe him. It is only now that I realise I can't get down, while Billy drops two branches and simply pushes himself from the tree, landing in a neat and silent crouch. The following moments are just seconds but that is all it takes for the nervousness to bring on the sickness. I begin to shake and mumble so much that Billy climbs the tree again and once more offers a big tablet with some more of his mother's advice.

Despite Billy's enthusiastic coaxing it is another fifteen minutes before I have summoned enough courage to relinquish my grip on the trunk, my behaviour becoming so erratic that upstairs lights begin to turn on in bedrooms up and down the street. Eventually, after much goading from Billy, I am prised out of the branches. I am sure I would have been able to descend quicker had he not kept grabbing for me with stunted fingers. I guess I should thank Billy for his help but I don't - I hunch up my shoulders, trying to blot him from my peripheral vision. I do not say goodbye, but begin to march back in the direction of my house. For the first time for as long as I can remember I will be genuinely pleased to be safely back amongst the rotting silence of my parents' crumbling relationship.

"You wanna go to the park and climb trees on Saturday?"

I ignore the question; my mind overturns, leaving nothing but the screech and drone of white noise. I am walking quickly but the anchor of Dorothy slows my escape. All the while this boy loiters behind me and I feel a wave of annoyance each time his extended shadow sweeps over me.

"I get out from about eleven. W-We can go fishing. You like fishing?"

Something about this boy's proximity is enveloping and suffocating and I fear that unless I can somehow prise his proximity from my clothes and skin, he will simply follow me into the house. For want of any intelligent thought, I am forced to turn and confront his harrying presence. It was as though he had not even noticed I'd stopped, slowing only slightly. While the scream remains trapped and stunned within my skull he has stepped closer, pressing with a smooth fluidity against me. I vibrate from the intrusion of a hand at my hip. It is more the image of his face obscuring the street light than the paralysing sensation of his mouth pressed to my skin that finally enables me to articulate the horror. He has missed my mouth, latching warm, moist lips to the point where my upper lip meets my cheek. They are there for only a moment before I jerk away, my claw raised in preparation to strike. But as my body tenses I involuntarily dislocate, leaving me to study the frozen figure in front of me. He remains leaning forward, jaw extended, pouting with his eyes closed. I pull away further but my gaze remains transfixed on this boy, still struggling to understand his intentions. Yet for some reason I struggle to maintain my anger; something about the incompetent comedy of my attacker is inherently disarming. Also, I am increasingly

128

conscious of the implications of my response. I have dislocated right in front of him. His eyes remain closed but I have dislocated while in direct physical contact with him. As such, it is inconceivable that it will remain undetected.

I study him, racking my brains for a plausible means of escape, fighting the revulsion of what I must do when the oxygen in my lungs depletes to the point I can no longer withstand its absence. Finally, reluctantly, I inch forward, pressing my hip back into the cup of his palm, pushing my face towards Billy's. I cannot tell you why, but at the last moment, I twist slightly - perhaps it was just momentary disgust in the idea of him drooling down my cheek. Here, I pause, my eyes open, his face little more than a dark blur of vague features.

I exhale and the moisture and warmth of Billy's mouth is back. I hear that people kiss with tongues; if he tries this I am sure to bite his face. My parents used to do this, kiss that is, though now I would not be entirely surprised if they started biting each other. But thankfully his lips remain closed, passively pushed against my own, painfully lingering as though expecting something to happen. It is now I who remains statuesque, my arms placed defensively across my flat chest while Billy shuffles slightly, retaining his balance.

The kiss is not as bad as I had feared but the encroaching hand that now curls into the small of my back ignites firecrackers of panic, causing me to tremble, passing the threshold of all I can feasibly tolerate. I vaguely recall emitting some high-pitched squeak as I pull away; Billy also jumps back, as though I am electrified. For one horrified moment I fear he will try and kiss me again and I retreat further, pulling Dorothy between us to shield my escape. But the boy does not renew his assault. Though there is little more than a yard's distance between us he begins to wave, yelling goodbye before turning to start running down the centre of the darkened street. His arms flap loosely as he passes under the streetlamps.

XXIV

The floor has been polished religiously and reflects the light like the surface of a grease-smeared mirror. It is made of rich dark wood, inducing a satisfying click from the heels of women's shoes while allowing the various wheelchairs and trolleys to glide as silently as a swan on water. When I walk on it in my trainers it squeaks, and for a number of minutes I grind the balls of my feet into the surface. Otherwise, the surroundings are cheap and bland. Cheaply-framed works of art hang from whitewashed walls. These are chocolate box scenes of mountains and streams, and romanticised images of country folk tilling the land. Soporific music is piped through small speakers mounted high into the corners of the room. The volume is so quiet I doubt most of the shuffling occupants are even aware of it. It is only because I have been standing here for a few minutes that I even notice it myself. Now, attuned to the various fluttering flutes and the bray of violins I can hear it clearly. It is a melody I have heard before, something modern, rinsed clean, rehashed and recycled for the most insipid of audiences. The flowers look fresh because they are made of either silk or plastic.

The walk from my house took longer than I expected and despite the cold my body feels warm and clammy. In addition to this, this place is unduly warm and it is beginning to make me feel faint. To sort myself out before my visit I lurk in the bathroom, constantly resisting the temptation to pull the long red cord which hangs down from the ceiling. There is no window, just an overzealous extractor fan which seems to be trying to suck every atom from the rectangular space. The walls are made of the same material as the floor, a heavy duty plastic that has begun to discolour from the endless washing of industrial detergents. The air is saturated by a throat-burning blend of bleach and lilies of the valley.

As I step from the bathroom my return immediately rings alarm bells in the overweight receptionist. Our stereotypes form hasty conclusions in each other as soon as I reappear. Hers: the potential threat of some feral youth, a dangerous menace to the quiet and fragile dispositions of her elderly patrons. Mine: the overbearing, underachieving bitterness that manifests itself in the petty obstinacy of bureaucrats. I prepare to be either patronised or dismissed without comment. I know she has been watching the door since I went in, no doubt imagining the numerous outrages or acts of antisocial behaviour I might have committed while the door was locked. Luckily for her I have already completed my quota of criminality for today: I stole some flowers earlier, as much as a prop in my role as a loving relative as a gift. My intrigue in the red cord was sufficient to make me not consider writing 'Francis Kelly eats shit' across the wall.

"Can I help you?"

The receptionist is craning her neck over the dispatch driver still grappling with some cumbersome delivery. She tries to be polite but either her contempt is too great or she is just not a particularly good actor.

"Mr Parker, Mr Derrek Parker. I have come to visit him."

I expect a challenge but none comes. In the following silence I watch the battle in the back of her mind.

"You on your own?"

I affirm this but the woman is clearly far from satisfied.

"Shouldn't you be at school?"

I tell the receptionist I am on compassionate leave. I resist the temptation to be sarcastic and my humility pays off. The woman snorts with derision and nods me in the direction of the only set of double doors which leads into the rest home.

"Barnerby Suite, first floor."

I don't suppose it matters too much to Derrek but the Barnerby Suite is not the most salubrious of dwellings. It is so bland, in fact, that I am surprised anyone bothered giving it a

131

name. Whoever Barnerby was, I doubt they could possibly be pleased with the association. The neat order from the reception has slipped, but the dull formulaic interior remains. The Suite is dominated by a large common room filled with numerous padded chairs arranged in a half moon around an aged television mounted on a creaking metal trolley. The volume is turned down, presumably for the benefit of the few patrons weighed down by thick blankets. All of them are women, all are asleep or as close as to render the difference meaningless. Other entertainments are tokenistic. There are ornaments and magazines, presumably more for visitors, and on one table sits a light scattering of jigsaw pieces which have probably not been moved for years. Two corridors lead from this space: one leads back to the staircase and reception, the other to the rows of dormitory style bedrooms. The piped music does not penetrate this far and for me, at least, this is a blessing. I cannot locate Derrek in the communal area but eventually find him seated by a small single bed in private quarters, probably as much to prevent his ramblings as out of any sense of privilege.

He seems much smaller than before. The nursing staff have taken the time to dress him, but his clothes no longer seem to fit. His eyes follow my arrival but there is no discernible emotion to suggest he either recognises me or is in any way affected by my presence. Part of me had expected this to be just such a non-event. Whoever dressed him did not take the time to brush his hair, the floating wisps of grey stand on end, projecting an image of eccentricity or derangement which is out of keeping with the bewildered features beneath. In the absence of a comb I find myself running my fingers through the tufts, curling locks behind large ears, more as a policy of containment than any meaningful styling.

The conversation consists solely of what I have to offer, and having little natural ability in small talk, I soon run out of things to say. This one-sided dialogue is the sum total of the words that have passed between us, and without Mrs Parker's interpretation I can draw no conclusion as to what, if anything, Derrek makes of my visit. My questions remain

132

unanswered and only so many of them can be rhetorical before I find that I am no longer talking at all, finding it more economical to simply conduct the morose monologue in the confines of my own head. The narrative is much as it is with Dorothy, and without the aid of an occasional yank on his collar I do not feel I am retaining whatever remains of Derrek's attention.

"Derrek? Derrek, can you hear me?"

I have to ask the question two more times before his eyes flicker and he slowly raises his head. Derrek bites his lower lip and from his repeated blinks it is clear he is seeing me for the first time. He smiles, but this just makes me feel sad and the futility of it all makes me question why I have come here. Certainly, nobody has asked me to and I do not imagine Derrek would have expected it. The funny thing is, I guess I came as much for the dog as I did for Derrek or out of respect for Mrs Parker. That and the realisation that I had little else to do.

"Ah, Mr Parker, you have a visitor. Lovely. Cup of tea?"

The comment comes from a passing nurse. I dread to think what she has been doing but she wears thick rubber gloves and a transparent plastic apron that is flecked with grey spittle. Only the beaming smile, her shoulder and short fingers curled around the door frame, are visible. Yet the cheeriness of her intervention is totally alien to our surroundings and when challenged by such good nature even I feel a vague desire to reciprocate. From the briefest glimpse of a fleshy hip I can determine that she is a great curvaceous woman, probably of a similar weight to the sullen receptionist, but able to retain some core energy that makes her bristle with purpose. This is a woman who seems out of sorts from her surroundings. She has retained something of herself, remained blissfully ignorant of the moribund decay that has saturated this entire building. More alarming still is that she seems genuine, lacking the false injection of patronising joviality. This is a place of lost time, faded memories, and death, yet she seems not to care. Such an existence seems deeply alarming, requiring a state of mind more in need of correction than my own. I do not really like tea but ask for a cup anyway. Simply so I know this woman will return, offering me another few seconds respite from Derrek's obliviousness.

After the nurse leaves I am forced to admit defeat, and what remains of Derrek's attention drifts away to the murky blanket of grey cloud beyond the window. I relinquish the idea of Derrek as an old man and replace it with Derrek the yet-to-be-allocated metaphor. I guess this is what it is like for Dr Attwood when sat across from me in our sessions. She finds herself sat in front of some curiosity, some approximation of a girl that generates questions but offers no insight or meaning. My observation and analysis only leads to more questions: does he miss Mrs Parker? Does he even remember her?

I wonder if he went to the funeral and, if he did, whether he understood what was happening? I wonder whether, if I brought him the dog, some neuron might fire, some sliver of synaptic input might finally connect to offer a flash, a momentary fragment of his past life, for old times' sake.

Prior to my visit I had walked past his previous home. Unseen forces have moved quickly to exploit his absence. The house has been stripped of possessions and a brightly coloured For Sale sign now stands proudly at the end of the increasingly unruly garden. As with Mrs Parker's funeral, I question who has orchestrated this; as far as I can recall, I know of no reference to them having any relatives. Do such things simply happen? Are clumsy mechanics in place to simply isolate and erase existences such as Mr and Mrs Parker's? The concept is not unduly distressing to me; these were, after all, just objects, objects which would conjure no sense of recall from the old man in front of me. Like Derrek they have been placed in storage, sealed away from what remains of a lingering consciousness. But unlike this man there is at least the slim prospect that some new relevance or memory may later become attached to them.

I look around the room for something to form the basis of a conversation; both the limited view from his window and the interior design offer nothing and my attention is finally drawn to the small cabinet by Derrek's chair. He makes no effort to prevent me rifling through its contents and after only a few minutes I am satisfied that there is little which is not stamped as property of the care home.

For want of anything to do I dislocate, but as I study Derrek there seems little in the way of variance to the animated version. I hope he is gone completely, lost in some idyllic second childhood where he is not tortured by his continuing decay and loss. But as I breathe out, something in this vacated human shell ignites and he becomes suddenly alert to my movement. For once I have been sloppy, returning from my void with such discrepancy that even this bewildered old man has taken notice. To Derrek, it must have seemed as though some instantaneous, miraculous shift has occurred, his visitor disappearing and reappearing in that instant. For a second I am fearful, turning to the door half-expecting to be faced with some stunned look of horror from the jovial nurse. But only Derrek is my witness and, as I watch, a smile spreads slowly across his face, a mischievous grin as though revelling in our shared secret. I am confident he will soon forget what he has seen, but for this instant he is complicit in all my past crimes and misdemeanours.

I step to the door. The nurse is nowhere to be seen and those few slumbering patients remain hypnotised by the flickering television. I close the door, turning back to Derrek to offer a deep bow in preparation for my performance.

In my first dislocation I move across the room, the snapping jerk of Derrek's head to my new position generating a brief squeak of delight and a clumsy clapping of hands. For my next dislocation I re-materialise standing on the bed, balanced on one foot, my arms extended as though I am a ballerina. After reappearing on top of the wardrobe I move onto the second stage of my act. Now it is objects that instantly transport from one side of the room to the other, various objects of weight and size, all props in a magic trick of magnificent ability. For the finale it is Derrek himself who is transported, dragged across the room to find himself at the window, initiating a moment of surprise too brief for him to be sure he has moved at all, for in the next instant he is back on the far side of the room.

I find a personal release in this demonstration of my abilities, something purging and self-affirming, providing evidence that this is actually real and not some extensive delusion Dr Attwood has neglected to comment on. Eventually, it is Derrek who grows tired of my theatrics, his enthusiasm not so much waning as lost in the clamour of the hazy whispers of a lifetime of experiences. I imagine that his thoughts are like the sound moths make fluttering at the window, easily overwhelmed by the everyday noise and confusion. Requiring too much effort to prevent them from being drowned and forgotten.

There is a knock at the door and the nurse is back with a cream mug of sweet tea in each hand. While I drink the tea she smiles and fusses around Derrek, providing a running commentary to her actions in lieu of actual conversation. I try to stay out of her way, trying to disguise my laboured breath from the last of a series of demanding dislocations. But watching her, I am aware that something is niggling at the back of the nurse's mind. Somehow Derrek's room has become disordered in those few moments in which she had gone to fetch the drinks. Something is inherently wrong but she can't quite put her finger on it. Thankfully, she makes no accusations or incriminations. Instead she throws herself into her work in the same way I imagine she approaches all her labours, quickly returning each displaced object to its pre-ordained place. Only now does she stop to study me, commenting on how I appear a little flushed, and pressing a cool hand to my forehead.

"Are you his granddaughter?"

I say I am. It is a harmless lie as it both pleases the nurse and gives Derrek a conversation to observe, if not take part in. I also have already decided I will not be visiting him again. My concept of Derrek was only ever as an extension of Mrs Parker or the dog. With the old lady gone and the care home forbidding animals, it is thought he has become superfluous. Yet in that time, while I drink my tea and spin my tale of the loving grandchild, the room seems a happy enough place. By the time the nurse remembers her countless chores I have already resigned myself to my final departure. Whether he knows it or not, this is Derrek's opportunity to say good bye, to say whatever it is, if there is anything, he wants to. As the nurse makes her excuses and turns to leave I follow her to the door. I say nothing, only look back once, to dislocate and to steal Derrek's watch.

XXV

"Well," says my mother. "It did not write itself, did it?"

This is blindingly obvious, and had she been listening to my protestations to date, she would realise that this fact is not being contested. I guess I should be pleased that my lack of appetite is, for once, not the main subject of conversation. But my parents' continuous line of questioning has come full circle once again and, I am beginning to think, to clear my plate may offer the only feasible avenue of escape.

Up until twenty minutes ago, before the telephone rang, the family evening meal was much like any other: an unappealing plate of food and a battle of wills between me and the unstable alliance of my parents. Once again I had made a few conciliatory gestures, but my hopes that Dorothy might rally to my cause have proven to be a disappointment.

The behaviour of the animal is, in fact, little short of traitorous, and the creature has clearly sided with my mother. It took me ages to coax her under the table without my parents seeing, and now, after tentatively licking at a few morsels which I had allowed to fall from my plate, it is categorically refusing to eat. I am almost tempted to use this reluctance in defence for my own absence of appetite. Dogs are, after all, hardly renowned for their culinary expertise or discriminatory tastes.

But before we could even settle into our entrenched positions, the telephone began its shrill demand for attention. I had of course offered to take the call, but was overruled by my mother and, with a curse, my father heaved his heavy frame from the table.

"So, this was purely his idea?"

"Yes," I reply with exasperation. At no point have I deviated from my categorical denial, yet my parents are refusing to even consider that I might be telling the truth.

But their intransigence represents only a token contributor to the boiling frustration.

It appears the telephone call was from Billy Rowley's mother; a tearful and embarrassed exchange, hoping to shed some light on why her son, found by police high on the side of a railway bridge, was daubing the black brickwork with fluorescent yellow paint.

This is an incident that would be mildly comical, were it not for the fact that I appear to be the misfortunate muse for his heartfelt declaration. For now, visible over the neat line of workmen's cottages that nestle along Skippons Street, the following words can be read: FrANSIS – 4 – BiLLy.

"And you did not put him up to it?"

"Mum, why would I put him up to this? Why would I want this written anywhere?"

"You have done similar things before."

This, I maintain, is both inaccurate and unfair. I do not deny that there have been instances of graffiti and vandalism in my past. But, I would like to think that I have put such occurrences behind me, and even if I had not, this current defacing of railway property in no way matches my usual modus operandi. All my previous acts of criminal damage have been both discreet and modest. I would also like to think that they demonstrated a distinct style and aesthetic, which is clearly missing in this instance.

"Mum, I swear I did not do this. Do you not think that, had I wanted my name written across a bridge, I would have spelt it correctly?"

My father is, at least, nodding in recognition of the point. My mother, however, is not letting this go. Her features are dark and mistrustful.

"Where were you this afternoon, Francis?"

"Out."

"Out where?"

I do not answer. Instead I condense myself into a ball, shutting down. I am now shivering, vibrating with unvented frustration. It is though this boy is the equivalent of a

139

biblical plague, his every action resulting in some infuriating and troublesome mishap. I am not so paranoid to think this might be the result of some intelligent design, rather, I liken it to the analogy of a clumsy dog, creating mayhem when it wags its tail. In this instance, a semi-illiterate proclamation that is now visible across the town's skyline. I do not doubt this slogan will soon be replicated, spawning fresh variations on the numerous slight and insults against me. I shudder to think how many lipsticks they will get through.

"Look," continues my mother, her voice softer, as though in appeasement. "We are pleased that you have a friend."

"He is not my friend."

My mother tries to look sympathetic, but her tone is patronising.

"It is only natural that young people explore their feelings. But it is important to be considerate when expressing these emotions."

"He's not my fucking friend."

"Francis!"

My father slams his cutlery against the dinner table.

"And I have no fucking feelings."

I exclude anger, of which the majority is at present focused, like cross-hairs, on the imbecilic face of Billy Rowley.

"How many times have we warned you about your language?"

"Fuck off."

"Get to your room!"

I do not argue, relishing the opportunity to escape both the meal and the conversation. I understand that such banishments are the stock trade of most parents. Yet, as a punishment, I remain wholly impervious to such tactics. In fact, the majority of my parents' perceived leverage is ineffective, and I remain indifference to their threats. Even the embarrassment of

Billy's message of devotion is not particularly embarrassing. It is the inquisition and the attention that it has created that I find most abhorrent, forcing me into awkward social interactions at which, I think you will agree, I am totally inept.

My 'walk of shame' is conducted in silence apart from the chink of cutlery on diner plates. There is no conversation between my parents and I wonder whether my outburst, and enforced absence, will result in another argument. I would like to think they might recognise the commonality of my association, taking solace in the small crumb of comfort that they are not alone, and at least one other person in the world shares their misfortune.

But on entering my room my mood lightens immediately. For there, sitting quietly on my bed, is Mrs Parker.

"Oh, hello," I say, brushing some soil off the bedsheets to sit next to her.

Mrs Parker does not turn. She stares blankly ahead, her empty eyes staring beyond her reflection in my bedroom window. For the next half hour I join her in her silent vigil, allowing my temper to cool, enjoying the solitude of her respectful company. It is a clear night and despite the light reflecting off the glass, we watch the slow ascent of the moon, its deflated shape adding a sense of cleanliness to the clutter of dirty blinking lights in the town below. Though it is a nice night, it is also a pity that it is not raining. I am sure, now that she is dead, Mrs Parker might have enjoyed a few hours racing raindrops. Such a distraction would have covered over the crack of my limited experience of hosting company.

I also look uncomfortably about the state of my bedroom. The squalor has not yet reached the point at which I will initiate another purge, but it is far from sanitary. Not that I personally care, but I imagine Mrs Parker would be sensitive to such matters; her own house, apart from her own corpse, was fastidiously tidy. Though, in keeping with Mrs Parker's agreeable character, if she has any objections she does not mention them. In this respect she is a courteous and respectful guest.

"Boy trouble?"

The question makes me snort with derision.

"You heard the discussions downstairs then?" I reply, and though Mrs Parker does not move, I imagine her nodding her head solemnly.

"Do you want to talk about it?"

"Not really."

"OK," Mrs Parker concedes, but she continues anyway. "They have their moments, I guess, but experience leads me to believe that men are burdensome creatures. It is one of life's cruel jokes that we must endlessly seek to foster these relationships. Even when there is nothing but good intention, like Billy, like my husband, they are ultimately just tiresome distractions. Though in fairness, I suspect that they could say the same of women."

I find myself imagining the scene below my feet: my father, having already wolfed down his meal, now waits impatiently for my mother to finish. There is a flat sadness to the scene.

"Something else to look forward to, eh?"

"Not really. There are instances of happiness, I guess, many of which are the defining moments of your life. And if you have aspirations of children, there is also the unfortunate necessity. But, for the endless trial and effort, it all seems so insubstantial."

I realise she is talking about Derrek, probably skirting around the main thrust of her disquiet, but I have no desire to press the issue. I try to keep the conversation going, but I am not well skilled in conversation, and as there is little in my life which is not either solitary or unpleasant, struggle for a new topic of mutual interest. It must be conceded that, apart from the bus stop and her death, we do not have that much mutual history.

Thankfully, Dorothy comes to my aid, pushing the door open with her nose to waddle slowly into the room. Usually I have to carry her up the stairs, but the effort is not beyond her. I guess she too has fled the moribund scene of my parents' marriage. But while she allows me to pick her up and place her between us, she remains oblivious to her previous owner, seemingly satisfied to curl into a ball and begin her rasping snores.

"School still tough?" she asks, but does not wait for a reply. "You're going to be OK, Francis."

I don't know what prompted the comment, but is good to hear. For the past few days I have become increasingly concerned. The vacuum of my indifference has corrupted, mutating into an insipid, creeping melancholy, breeding self-pity, which I dislike intensely.

"You know what you need to do, you just need the courage of your conviction."

"Are you sure?"

"I'm certain, Francis."

"But…"

"No buts, Francis."

Once again I have a strong desire to change the subject.

Listening in silence, I hear the front door open and shut, and shortly after the engine of our car. The headlights obliterate our reflections in the glass, casing a sweeping beam to rotate shadows through the room. I guess it is my father who has gone out, but the silent house below my feet offers no clue.

"Your parents are under a lot of pressure," continues Mrs Parker. "Try not to be hard on them. They are good people, but they can't help you. The same can be said of your teachers, Francis. They mean well, but they are simply incapable of understanding, and if they can't understand, they cannot serve your best interest. But I guess you already know this."

Regardless, it is good to hear someone else articulate my thoughts.

"And Dr Attwood?" I ask, again anticipating the answer.

"Especially Dr Attwood, Francis. Of all the people you know, it is she who must be dealt with the most caution. She is dangerous for you, you must proceed with extreme care."

"You think I should skip her sessions."

"Perhaps, if you think she suspects, certainly."

I am about to ask whether Mrs Parker would come with me to one of Dr Attwood's sessions, but the old woman anticipates the question.

"Probably best you don't mention me, Francis," says Mrs Parker. "She is not going to understand."

The truth is so obvious I simply nod in agreement.

"But the girls in my class?"

I imagine Mrs Parker waving her hand as though to dismiss the objection.

"They only have power over you because you allow them to. And any power that you can simply choose to take away, is no power at all. I swear to you, Francis, a moment's courage is all it will take, and then you will never have to think of them again. But I admit, if you offer them nothing but passive inaction, they will, ultimately, destroy you."

In the lull in conversation, our attention turns back to the window. A bedroom light in one of my neighbour's houses has been turned on, the curtains have yet to be drawn and we are offered a momentary insight into the workings of a stranger's life. Most of this small stage is a view of the opposing green painted wall, illuminated by the single light that hangs over the sole actor's head. Living so close to us, I have seen this man numerous times before, but have rarely spoken to him. I guess he is the same age as my father. But he seems older due to the significant grey in his hair. He is also significantly fatter than my father. Judging by his movement it can be assumed he navigates around a sizable bed, repeatedly picking clothing from a wardrobe that lurks just out of my eye line. Obliviously unaware that he is being scrutinised, there is an almost clandestine feeling to his behaviour, but without the narrative or sound, his actions look staged and rehearsed. Despite them being such monotonous and simple tasks, he seems ponderous, so much so that it is beginning to irritate me. Finally he stops, and stands looking over the objects he has laid on the bed, scratching his head as though bamboozled by the array laid out before him.

"Do you think he's choosing his suit for the morning?" I ask.

"I'm dead, Francis," comes Mrs Parker's factual reply, "just a voice in your head. I am an illusionary idea, I can't tell you anything you don't already know."

The observation, is well made, and leaves me with a lot to think about.

XXVI

I am not very good at lying. Certainly not good enough to match Dr Attwood's skilful inquisition. Initially, in the first of our sessions, I was unprepared and unaware of her strategies, allowing myself to be led into numerous psychological bottle necks and emotional ambushes. Even now, months later, though the line of our discussions has moved on, the information I naively surrendered in those early incursions still comes back to haunt me, and I have yet to fully recover and repair the damage of these initial raiding parties. Worse still, I feel I have since compounded these errors with amateurish efforts to set false trails of breadcrumbs. Again, I was underestimating the skill of the doctor, revealing more and more of myself than I had ever intended.

Not that I consider her some sort of adversary or nemesis, but I do dislike the probing nature of her questions. I will even begrudgingly admit that Dr Attwood is, within the parameters of her own understanding, trying to help me. And, when considering the base material which is Francis Kelly, she has her work cut out for her.

With the realisation that I am an exceedingly poor liar, I have at least been able to defend an exposed flank. Before, I would lie about many things, say stupid things, tell small and silly lies which bordered on the pathological due to the lack of necessity. And Dr Attwood would smile and take notes, the conversations would move on to other seemingly innocuous topics and I would leave our weekly sessions oblivious to the traps I had laid for myself. In some instances it was weeks before I was even aware that I was becoming entangled in a web of my own making. The doctor was supremely patient, and she was careful not to show her full hand. The initial lies, buried away in the paper files, would periodically resurface, raised at unexpected moments, unbalancing me, leading to clumsy and hasty elaborations, elaborating on an unsustainable narrative which, increasingly obvious to both of us, was little more than a blatant fabrication.

Yet Dr Attwood never challenged me directly, never once wearily put down her pen and paper to stare accusingly at me. At no point did she ever brand me a bare-faced liar. It was left to me to do the job for her, to either admit the attempted deceit or ignore my contradictions to offer some other insipid concoction of half-truths and timid confessions. This only heralded the beginning of my torments as Dr Attwood probed for greater understanding under the disguise of sympathetic concern. I was asked to explain why– why I had lied, exploring the rationale for my duplicity. This invariably led to further questions. To each question I used to try some defining and definitive statement, hoping to terminate the conversation and her line of enquiry. Inevitably, these would only serve to sink me further into the quicksand of endless analysis.

Instead of lying, I now base my strategy around simply not engaging or talking at all. Here, Dr Attwood has demonstrated herself to be an efficient and competent opponent, able to tolerate my aloof silence and unquantifiable gestures with greater skill than the vast majority of people. While the doctor waits for me to speak, I suspect she is drawing some conclusions, but by limiting my exposure through passive and laconic statements she is unable to test them with much satisfaction. Key to my strategy is the understanding that our sessions are time-critical, the clock on the wall allowing me to give structure to my defence, knowing that time is increasingly against her, increasingly threatening to conclude yet another unsatisfying personal audience with Francis Kelly without any tangible benefit. Yet I suspect that Dr Attwood charges by the hour so she cannot complain about the relative ease at which she earns her wages.

It would be interesting to know what proportion of our sessions are conducted in total silence, for even when I speak I do so with a slow and ponderous deliberation. On many occasions I simply stop mid-sentence to leave them unfinished, or begin a new, wholly

unrelated comment. I am confident that Dr Atwood struggles with this strategy. She writes

less notes than she did in our earlier sessions and rarely seeks to unpick or explore these

incomplete utterances. Instead of lying, I have manufactured a rambling, fractious monologue

which fills many minutes but is wholly void of any meaning.

The other mainstay of my defence is, I admit, a little childish, but it is a simple retort.

As much to play for time, I obtusely reiterate the same question Dr Attwood has asked me. If

nothing else, this is a source of frustration for Dr Attwood but it also serves to waste a few

more seconds. She reminds me that it is I who am the subject of the therapy, and that her

responses to the question are ultimately irrelevant. But to me this just seems highly

unsatisfactory and a little disingenuous. If my improvement in her sessions is based upon the

correct answer to these questions then, were the doctor to give me a hint - an approximation

of what a normal, healthy person would reply - this would seem an obvious way of

developing some momentum. These endless cryptic riddles are not helping anyone.

This eventually leads to the same debate. She asks me whether I trust her. I do not

mean to appear evasive but I find this is a far from simple question to answer and again I find

this is a question best answered with another question. Do I trust her? This of course depends

on what exactly it is that she is doing. It is also a question that I could just as easily ask the

doctor. She has no need for such dependence - it is I, after all, who has come, or more

accurately has been sent, to her therapy sessions.

"Do you think we are progressing, Francis."

This is one of the questions I remain silent to. But this is not stubbornness, rather the

silence is genuine, primarily because I don't really understand the question. To my mind this

is also not a question for me to answer. It is other people, such as my parents and the doctor,

who have decreed I have a problem, and I remain ignorant as to whether I am getting better or worse. Ultimately, it seems to me, it is other people who decide this shift in position. Perhaps this is a question Dr Attwood should be answering as I have no idea - I am not entirely sure what we are even supposed to be progressing towards. Do I feel rehabilitated? Do I feel that I am better, healthier, and more compatible with the template of the average fourteen-year-old girl? Does Francis work? And what if I do? I am under no illusion that an opinion of miraculous recovery would be dismissed by Dr Attwood and would not find me free from these hourly sessions.

"Well, Dr Attwood," I might say, "I feel much better, thank you."

To this, do you think for one second Dr Attwood might look up from her notepad and nod her head in agreement?

"Through your patient support," I might continue, "I have successfully realigned my perspective. I now feel balanced, open and responsive, strong enough to not only cope, but to also thrive in society. Now, after overcoming my initial resistance, and after fully engaging with you in these sessions, committing to the various medical interventions you have prescribed for me, I am sufficiently conscious of my emotional and psychological needs. Thank you, Dr Attwood, thank you so much."

I do not imagine the doctor smiling, putting down her notepad and pen and rising to shake my hand. I do not expect her to accept my diagnosis, to usher me to the door, launching me like some chick from the nest into the wider world. Such an opinion would only lead to countless additional questions, committing me to many more hours of therapy as Dr Attwood systematically challenges and deconstructs my delusions. Presumably, as I am still here, I have not been progressing, and I am for all intents and purposes still a significant distance from my intended destination. I am, of course, presuming that Dr Attwood knows the answer to her own questions. So why is she asking me?

XXV

Do I want another doctor? Do I want a doctor at all? I can't deny that there is something wrong with Francis, and that without some form of outside interference her future looks increasingly bleak. Something in her mechanism is simply not working as it should, but I am increasingly convinced that a doctor is not the answer. Neither Dr Attwood nor any of her predecessors have come close to locating the defect, the rusted cog or spring which is holding back the entire assembly line.

In some ways I would even go so far as to say that they have made matters worse. It is as though each in turn has taken poor Francis apart to see what is wrong with her. Each has then put her back together, finding only as they close the lid that she is just as defective as before, and now there are a few more parts left over which they never found a home for. Francis is not a car, a mechanic and some new parts and a bit of fine tuning is not going to have her purring smoothly. Though perhaps this is unfair, as I recognise that the analogy might hold true. With a car you can simply keep replacing parts, a bolt here and a spring there. You can add new tyres or a new coat of paint. Oil is changed regularly and you can wash and wax the vehicle every other Sunday. If the car does not work you just keep going, keep swapping one bit for another. If you take this to an extreme, in the end, you have reached the point where you no longer have any of the original car you started with. Whether you still want to call your car Francis at this point is up to you.

XXVII

The sun is out, offering a small taste of spring, which is still many weeks away. The sunshine does coax some colour from the monochromatic world, but the clear skies leave it bitterly cold. Despite this, an executive decision has been taken somewhere in the higher echelons of the school administration, and the entire congregation have been shooed from the various block-like buildings, to soak up some vitamin D.

To me, the scene could be likened to that of some prison yard. The faded lines of tennis courts are laid out on the grey tarmac, but there are no nets, and nobody can ever remember any games being played. Around this open expanse loops a sturdy wall of crumbling breeze blocks. These have been painted in various places with white emulsion, presumably to cover some graffiti, but now giving the impression that the wall is being treated for chicken pox. Above this there is a rusted chain-linked fence that catches litter and plastic bags that roll across this open space like tumble weeds.

Only the younger children play, as much to keep the warmth in their bodies as through any sense of entertainment. The sullen ranks of my classmates form into clusters of their peers, huddling like chickens, ducking the numerous footballs which are repetitively punted from one end of the yard to the other. They chatter like geese, creating a screaming cacophony of adolescent voices and bleeping telephones; wisp-like plumes of breath are carried away on the biting breeze. Even if I knew who any of these people were I would struggle to recognise them, as all are wrapped in scarves and thick padded jackets.

The only other objects are a few recycling bins and, as the only cover, it is by these large plastic domes that I have been loitering, stamping my feet to fight the cold and feeling my face flush pink from the exposure. This is a prime location to study the shifting mass of bodies and, like some timid antelope caught isolated on the open plain, I constantly scan the crowd for potential predators.

One figure does continually catch my attention. For some reason I now seem to see Billy Rowley everywhere, leading me to conclude that he is a new addition to the school. I am sure, even without the regrettable encounters to date, I would have noticed him had he been at the school for more than a few weeks. This is because he runs everywhere. This is not simply a consistent jog, and there is no sense of economy. He literally sprints, chaotically, and with a continuous desperation, as though fleeing for his very life.

Even now I can track his mazy path through the huddled knots of figures. He is contained only by the breeze blocked walls, ricocheting like some pinball, to set off again in a new, random direction. He jumps as he runs, his arms flailing as though trying to communicate by semaphore, apparently indifferent to the elements as he wears no gloves and his jacket is left to flap open. I think he yells something as he runs but, at this distance, whatever utterance he makes is lost amongst the multitude. Then, for no obvious reason, he will stop dead, tense and alert like some confused spaniel responding to a dog whistle. But this pause is only momentary as, having received some secret new instruction, he is off again, racing between the huddled groups, kicking satchels and knocking over my smaller classmates. It makes me both cold and fatigued just to look at him.

On other days, I have observed him climbing up the fence, displaying significant agility to invert himself, hooking his feet over the lip, to hang like some gigantic bat. This has brought numerous rebukes from the school staff and janitors, complaining at the deep impressions he leaves on the fence as much as the risk to his personal safety.

I must admit that he is becoming an object of curiosity. But to date I have avoided the temptation for a closer inspection through dislocation, choosing instead to maintain a secretive distance to watch his frantic ramblings through the school premises. The boy also deeply disturbs me, and I remain convinced that his antics are part of some wider, nefarious strategy. A devious scheme, of which I am some critical, yet unwilling, component.

Significant reanalysis of our past encounters has failed to draw any evidence of method to his madness. But what is clear is that, for some unknown reason, I am the fearful subject of his interest. On more than one occasion he has sought to catch my attention, waving and, worse still, hollering my name down crowded school corridors. In such instances my escape had required risky dislocations, deploying evasion tactics I have previously reserved for my nemesis and her cohort of lackeys.

Know your enemy, I mutter into my scarf, stiffening my resolve to ensure I am not distracted by either the tedium or the cold.

But now I realise that I have been losing perspective, recognising that this boy, and his lunatic antics, border on a luxury when compared with the ever-present threat of a good kicking. In this instant I recognise I am dangerously exposed, and have stayed stationary for too long. I am no longer confident that this is a wise place to stand. The low winter sun forces me to squint my eyes. It casts long shadows, making it difficult to differentiate between the potential persecutors and those who remain entirely indifferent to my existence.

"Guess who?"

For the briefest of moments I detected movement out of the corner of my left eye before I am enveloped from behind. Despite the weather, his bare hands are still warm and clammy, pressed solidly against my face. I instinctively twist to pull away, but for such a small boy he is incredibly strong.

"Fuck off, Billy!" I spit, thrashing to free myself, but the clamp around my face only tightens, and I can smell the sticky sugar on his fingers.

"Billy who?" comes the reply. I can almost hear the idiotic grin in his voice. "There are many boys called Billy in this school."

I flail my arm but can find no purchase; similarly, my efforts to rake his shins with my heel also fail to find their target. Only when I attempt to swing my head back in search of his nose is there any meaningful effect. No contact is made, but there is sufficient need for self-preservation for his grip to slip sufficiently so that I can twist myself free.

My attacker is smiling at me, and for one horrible moment I fear he is going to try and kiss me again. I screw my hand into a fist in anticipation, preparing to throw my minimal weight into Billy's jaw.

"What you doing?"

"None of your fucking business," I reply in outrage, but Billy just starts laughing, a high-pitched giggle that is irritating and disarming in equal measure.

"You want a sweet?" Billy asks, extending his open hand. The objects, if they are sweets, look like they have been in his pocket for some while. A couple of them look half eaten, and I can see that some of them are his medication.

"No."

"So, what are we going to play now?"

"Sorry?"

"What are we going to play, now that I have caught you, that is?"

It takes a moment to realise Billy's mistake, confusing my evasion as some longitudinal game of hide and seek, played out between lessons. For a brief moment I consider some cruel prank, to suggest Billy hides and then to pretend to close my eyes and begin my slow count to one hundred. I imagine him running away with frenetic delight, possibly remaining crouched in some secluded spot for the remains of the day, chuckling to himself, labouring under the belief that I might be scouring the school for him.

"You're really good. I thought I'd caught you this morning."

"Thanks."

"You ran into the girls' room in B-Block. I waited for ages, but you never came out. Did you climb out of the window?"

"I…"

"You want to climb some trees after school?"

"No."

"You want to go throw rocks in the canal?"

"No."

"You want to …"

The questions are coming quickly and with little appreciation for my response. That he is asking the questions, increasingly excited at the prospect of his pointless adventures, seems enough. He is indifferent to my flat refusals. Despite his manic running it is only now, as he rattles off question after question, that he begins to pant with exertion, as though his brain is struggling to keep up.

"You can bring your little dog, if you like."

Reference to Dorothy brings the possibility of some lame excuse, and I seize on it immediately.

"Sorry, Billy, my dog is old and unwell. I am taking her to the vets."

He accepts this obvious lie, meekly and without comment. But he continues to watch me hungrily, fidgeting with some barely restrained energy. He blinks a number of times and bites at his lower lip before clumsily stepping forward. I step backwards, knocking over some discarded drink can with my heel.

"Billy, look," I say, more out of appeal than with any conviction. I can feel the sickness returning, a nausea which leaves me weak and brittle, extenuated by the biting cold. There is a growing pressure within my skull, inducing a violent vibration and causing my head to spin. My mouth fills with saliva, so much so that I must repeatedly swallow to

155

prevent myself from choking. This in turn forces me to fight for breath, and I feel the flux of time pulsating against my skin as I hover at the cusp of dislocation.

"Wait," I cry. Billy has lurched forward again, grasping out to take hold of my hand. Flinching, I pull back further, pressing my arms to my flat chest, hiding my hands under my armpits.

"Shall I walk you home after school?"

"Yes!"

My words come out as an anguished cry of desperation, the illness turning into physical panic. I long to flee but no longer trust my limbs to keep me standing, let alone escape. Billy, I know, will surely pursue, again misinterpreting my attempt at escape for some new manifestation of a game, which only he is playing. The thought of his grabbing me again is simply too much to bear.

"Yes?"

His fists are clenched, as though about to raise his arms in celebration.

"Yes, after school," I croak, all the while slowly retreating backwards, until my back presses into the wall. Thankfully, my concession has arrested his approach, his face now contorting as though struggling to comprehend the implications of my acceptance.

"OK," he says. He is smiling but now suddenly unsure of himself, and I watch his mouth chew over his thought, as half- formed phrases die on his lips.

"See you later, then," I say, summoning as much authority as the sickness will allow, hoping to terminate the conversation. It hardly needs stating that I have absolutely no intention of honouring my commitment.

Although we are standing only a yard apart, Billy waves at me before leaving, turning to once more sprint away, as though in mortal flight. Only now, as his fleeting form

156

disappears amongst my peers, can I begin to wrestle back control of my emotions, drawing deep breaths of ice old air, which chills my body.

I turn to the sound of the snigger, and my heart stops. Rebecca Shiels is standing on the other side of the wall, her brightly coloured finger nails hooked like talons into the chains of the fence. She has seen and heard everything, and is barely able to contain her delight.

"Liking your new boyfriend, Kelly. I guess this is what happens, for people like you. The freaks form their own little cluster. Left to scratch about in the filth by the bins."

She screws her face up and makes rodent-like noises. There is a cold hatred to her glare, which I struggle to match.

Thankfully she is alone, having seemingly dispensed with the need for her toadying entourage. I recognise that this, and the fence that forms a natural barrier between us, means I am unlikely to take a beating. But this is of scant consolation and, as with many of the attacks, I find myself rooted to the spot, unable to form any clear thought process as to how best to defend myself. Strangely, I do recognise that the sickness has gone. It is as though, despite the threat, Rebecca does evoke a familiarity which I find more manageable that the alien and disconcerting presence of Billy Rowley. Though I acknowledge that this may just be the overwhelming response to my fear, inducing a paralysis, so that a heroic effort is required for even the simplest of movements.

"Freaks can't be picky, I guess," continues Rebecca, warming to her rhetoric, savouring my promised humiliation.

I want to feign indifference, but experience has shown how futile such an attempt would be. Rebecca knows that I am bluffing, and she enjoys watching me squirm as her barbed comments strike home.

"Do you sniff each other out deliberately, or just sort of gravitate to each other? Sticking together, like various pieces of shit?"

I try and ignore her.

"Look at me, you piece of shit!" hisses Rebecca.

I know I should just walk away, but the promise of the abuse, left looming over me, seems too much to bear. It is as though some masochistic part of me needs to know how this girl will use her new-found knowledge. Though I feel my resolve crumbling, I do at least keep my eyes turned, suddenly finding new interest in my badly scuffed shoes.

"Tell me, Kelly, what is he like in bed?"

I feel myself going red, and mumble some weak denial. Though my words are barely audible, they induce a hiccup of incredulity.

"Oh my God, you have, haven't you?"

For some reason, all I can think about is Billy kissing me, and my reluctant willingness to press myself back against his lips.

"Oh, this is priceless!" mocks Rebecca, though her laughter. "You and that chimpanzee. I am not even sure who gets the worst of it."

The bell goes to signal the end of break, and my classmates turn to file back into the buildings. The migration is slow but steady, the usual dissent and dislike of whatever class awaits them is crushed by a pragmatic desire for warmth. The grating chime also breaks my own inertia, offering the chance to flee from this poisonous inquisition. Yet my steps are shuffling and unsteady, as if I have forgotten how to walk, and my movements feel forced and contrived. On the other side of the fence, Rebecca shadows my movement, slapping at the chain fence for my attention.

"What is he like, Kelly? When he is between your legs, I mean. Are you not scared when he comes bounding towards you, waving his little maggot prick?"

I want to run, but muster the last of my restraint in the hope of retaining some small fraction of dignity. For a brief moment I even consider dislocating.

"Give it to me, Billy," Rebecca moans, mockingly.

I walk on in silence, tripping over my own feet.

"I want you, Billy. I want you inside me again."

I can feel myself shaking, not with the sickness but some aimless rage. I feel hot, the incandescent fury generating an intense heat that has driven the winter from my bones.

"Harder, Billy. Harder!" continues Rebecca, laughing. "I can picture the scene. I bet you two had to sit for hours working out what to do. Good job it is predominantly a matter of mimicking the diagrams, as I bet that idiot can't read. You probably had to show him what to do. Of course, you'd probably want to colour in the pictures first."

My chest lurches and I am forced to choke down my own vomit. Yet there is still no confusion.

"No, I've changed my mind. I bet he is fucking massive. I bet he has a cock like a donkey. I bet you are moistening up just thinking about it."

Something snaps in my head, a pronounced click, which leaves a high-pitched ringing in my ears and a stabbing pain at my temples.

"But I guess it is probably diseased and rotting now it has been near your grubby little snatch."

"SHUT. UP. YOU. SLUT." Each word is delivered with calm precision and control. But these are not my words. It is as though, from somewhere in my head, I have heard them spat from the dead mouth of Mrs Parker and I have just repeated them to devastating effect. I am confused. But not as much as Rebecca who stands blinking, her mouth frozen in a lopsided pout, her tongue pressed into her cheek and her fist held to the side of her face. The unbalancing is only momentary, but for this instant she is exposed. She blinks twice more as her rage gathers, setting her features with murderous hostility. The amorphous plumes of grey breath that hang between us are the only movement in a scene which is as still as any dislocation.

"What the fuck did you call me?"

I want to say it again, in my head a voice is screaming: slut, slut, slut, but the connection between my mouth and lungs is now cluttered with emotion. I open my mouth, hoping to press home some lingering advantage, but without Mrs Parker to guide me my effort is weak and faltering.

"You're fucking dead, Kelly!" snaps Rebecca, smashing both palms against the fence. "I'm going to fucking end you."

"Leave now, Francis," says Mrs Parker. Her voice is authoritative and I obey without thinking, turning on my heels to walk out across the school yard. The last of my classmates filter past me in the other direction, while behind me I can still hear Rebecca's threats.

"You're dead, Kelly."

"Walk slowly," says Mrs Parker, "take your time."

"You hear me, Kelly? You are dead!"

Mrs Parker tells me not to look back, but as I reach the gate I cannot help myself. The yard is now empty apart from discarded drink cans and crisp packets, and in a far corner I see a rucksack has been forgotten. Rebecca has not moved from the spot where I left her, and continues to glare menacingly, allowing her anger to conjure new and painful humiliations. Over such distance I could still have heard her, but instead of shouting she simply mouths the words, enunciating each syllable to leave no doubt as to their sentiment.

You – Are – Dead.

I find myself nodding in agreement, as I walk away.

A short spate of truancy simply delays the inevitable. I have deliberately excused myself from half a dozen lessons, but this has achieved nothing but for me to become more timid, and to presumably provide an opportunity for my persecutors to formulate some ingenious revenge. As such, my self-imposed exile has been somewhat self-defeating; though my attackers are in possession of many traits, I have seen nothing to suggest imagination is one of them.

Now, resigned to my fate, I make no great effort to hide my presence. I retain some lingering hope that the intensity of the violence might in some way be abated. But, in truth, I have long since come to recognise that, if it wasn't Mrs Parker's well-meaning intervention, they would soon be beating me up for something else.

Yet, I can't help think that in some way things have now changed between Rebecca and me, the nature of our last encounter having fundamentally altered the dynamics between us. Despite all the beatings, all the humiliations, with those four words Mrs Parker has sown a small seed of doubt, and it is now this girl who must impose herself. A chain of events have been initiated, potentially pushing us beyond the point of no return.

Despite Rebecca Shiels' words repeatedly echoing in my ears, I am somewhat surprised to find myself still inherently passive to the gathering threat. This is not indifference, but rather a sense of acceptance, as though cocooning myself from the threat is, in some small way, confirming that an insurmountable difference exists between us.

I am currently sitting in Mr Beckley's Maths class, another tired room of uniform rows of desks. Every surface seems covered in some durable industrial plastic. The room smells of detergents and liberally applied deodorant, the fumes combining to create a sickly-sweet mixture that catches the back of my throat. The tall windows allow much light to enter, but the view of the staff car park is insipid, even on a summer's day.

It is just as I finish colouring in a page of my geography text book that the second bell goes and, looking up, I notice that Mr Beckley has yet to arrive. Times like these are always dangerous for me. My classmates are already becoming restless, spurred on by the possibility that they have been forgotten: becoming disruptive and increasingly daring. There is a slow but steady escalation of misbehaviour in such instances. The small, grouped conversations, clustered around the room, slowly lose their structure. The volume increases as my classmates increasingly roam from their desks in search of entertainment. Despite the liberty of these unrestrained moments boredom comes quickly, and it is not uncommon for me, or some other unfortunate, to become the source of entertainment for one or more of my fellow pupils. As such, in such instances, it is safest for me to retreat from the class, to linger in the corridor. Thankfully, neither Rebecca nor Billy are in my mathematics class, and it is the thought of them stalking the corridors that makes me choose to stay crouched amongst my classmates.

As a point of interest, I have not dislocated since I last saw Rebecca. It is as though, with her looming vengeance hanging over me, time is dragging laboriously as it is, and there is little value in extending my stay of execution with more dead and timeless existence. The wait is inducing a vague weariness, though I admit this may just be a response to the stress of my predicament.

Mr Beckley is sure to arrive in any moment and, just as I think I am safe, the door swings open. My classmates momentarily flinch, caught in whatever misdemeanour would draw their teacher's rebuke. But it is not the slouched frame of my math teacher who fills the doorway. It is a girl roughly my own age who steps into the class, followed by her malodourous friends. She barely scans the room, fixing an intense stare in my direction.

"Oh, Francis," Rebecca coos. "Oh, my Juliet."

She is a master of stage management, and whatever it was my classmates were doing has been swiftly forgotten. Every pair of eyes is now following Rebecca's approach as she pick her way between the desks towards me.

"I have something for you, something from your lover boy."

Alison Townsend snorts with derision, and a couple of my classmates have already begun to giggle in anticipation of the comedy. From inside her blazer jacket Rebecca draws a small slip of paper, holding it with the tips of her manicured fingers, at the very corner.

"It seems," she announces, more to the class than to me, "Francis Kelly has an admirer."

The stunned incredulity of my classmates is marked, though entirely understandable. Though my attention never flinches from the incriminating evidence. Even from this distance I can see the disjointed handwritten note, the jagged letters, written in multi-coloured crayons.

The desk in front of me is free and it is here that Rebecca now looks to hold court, gathering her audience around her. She waves the paper at me like some handkerchief, mockingly allowing it to waft enticingly in front of my face. But I anticipate her intent, guessing she is hoping that I will clumsily reach for it, so she can snatch it away. It would be a simple enough dislocation to beat her to it, to gently pluck the sheet from her statuesque grip. Then, in an instant, it would be gone. But now over a dozen of my peers are staring intently at both me and the dangled sheet of paper. I am keenly watched from every perceivable angle.

Instead, I close my eyes, bracing myself for a public humiliation. But Rebecca is taking her time, allowing the anticipation to build and, in this moment, I form a mental image of what Rebecca has been doing for the past few days.

"To my darling Francis," Rebecca narrates, holding the note proudly in front of her like some great orator. "I long to hold you in my arms; to squeeze your tiny breasts."

The room erupts in laughter.

I imagine her having taken Billy to one side, probably on some pretext of being my envoy. I imagine the subtle manipulation, to the point that the written note becomes his idea and not hers, her control of this boy now so total that he does not even pause to think as she dictates the grammarless text. The sentiment is Billy's, but these words, the words I can hear over the chorus of braying laughter, are definitely hers. She pauses only to contain her own humour, reciting the increasingly crude monologue of past and promised sexual exploitations. But I do not focus on the words, choosing instead to listen to my own internal thought processes.

"Breathe, Francis," says Mrs Parker.

"And he's drawn a picture!" howls Rebecca, and there is a fresh scream of laughter as she holds up the image to the class. A crushed piece of paper, thrown from behind my back, strikes weakly against the side of my head.

"Are you breathing, Francis?"

"Yes, Mrs Parker."

"OK, take a deep breath…"

I fill my lungs to feel the tremor around me as time prepares to solidify.

"Exhale."

I do as commanded; the clamour of the noise around me is almost deafening. Rebecca is no longer reading.

"Breathe in."

"Yes, Mrs Parker."

"Fuck, imagine the children? The mongoloids would have to be kept in a zoo."

"Now hit the bitch."

I move slightly before I exhale, accelerating upwards from my chair. Rebecca's face has hardly twitched as my right hand arches in on its target. But it is an embarrassingly weak punch, flapping aimlessly against the top of her head. In an instant the communal joviality is gone, replace with the guttural roar of the bear pit, as I continue my assault. But the second attempt is as ineffectual as the first, and the retaliation is overwhelming. The blow does not come from Rebecca, still reeling from the initial punch. Instead, I feel the impact to my left side as the significant weight of Alison Townsend comes crashing into my flank, driving me from my chair. I land badly onto my shoulder, my head having caught the corner of the desk on the way down.

"You fucking bitch!" I hear; it is Rebecca's voice. The blow which accompanies it is not a punch, but the weight of her knee, landing onto my ribs. Sharp nails now grip at my skull, grabbing at my hair, to drive my head back against the cold classroom floor. What follows is a barrage of slaps and punches. But it is only when I find my jaw being forced open, and the hard mass of Billy's note being forced into my mouth, that I genuinely begin to panic.

"Eat it, you fucking freeeaaaaaakkkkkkkkkk.............."

The world slurs into a dislocation but the pain remain real, and though I gasp for air I cannot breathe. The lump of paper in my mouth seems as solid as rubber and though I push at it in desperation with my tongue, I cannot force this mass from my throat. It takes almost all my strength to suck air through my nose, fighting against the weight of the knee still pressed against my chest. But this momentary relief is woefully insufficient and, as my surroundings plunge back into the stagnant state of atrophy, I feel my body spasm, lurching in revolt, pleading for sustenance.

Choking, I push against the mass of Rebecca; she rises compliantly into the air, and her hand is no longer pressed over my mouth. Her frozen form hangs over me like some silent spectre. Her face is contorted with hate but I have more pressing concerns as I continue to gag on the crumpled ball of paper now lodged in my throat. I try to force my own fingers into my mouth, but find myself unable to reach sufficiently far to gain purchase. So in desperation I try to swallow, hammering my small fists silently against my chest to force the mass past my windpipe. In that moment I hear the cry of anguish in my head as panic takes over, and as I thrash I feel my strength and consciousness slipping from my grasp.

"No."

The single word is all I hear, a simple statement of fact, uttered from the still lips of a dead old woman. But, despite her objection, I can still not breathe. I feel the edges of the paper have become softer, more malleable, but at its core the dry lump continues to suffocate. With each effort to swallow comes a stabbing pain, the efforts of my limbs to kick away the obstructing mass now little more than a fevered vibration.

With one desperate last effort I wince against the pain as my throat crushes against the obstruction, forcing it to slip slightly before finally dislodging, squeezing over my chest with a deep bruising ache. But I can breathe, and with a croaking cry I stretch my diaphragm to allow the air to cascade into my damaged throat.

Time returns clumsily, and in a brutal instant the weight of Rebecca Shiels comes crashing down onto my prone body. She is unbalanced and left spread on top of me, kicking with her limbs against the startling effects of gravity and her own confusion. I think it is at this point that I lose consciousness.

166

XXVIII

The realisation that something has gone wrong comes slowly, like a whisper that you struggle to hear for minutes, and even when you locate the source of the voice you still cannot understand the words. Perhaps it was also the darkness that hid the realisation from me. I have wandered much farther than I normally do, the street lights are gone and the pale blue light of morning has yet to reveal much detail of the rolling countryside. My house is on the edge of town so I am not unduly worried. Nothing looks familiar and turning to look back from where I have presumably walked, I can see the distant polluting glow of the street lights, nightshifts at factories, and the headlights of vehicles. Soon more lights will blink into existence, first from bedrooms and then bathrooms, spreading through the suburbs and tower blocks. Another day.

My legs are caked with mud and my feet feel tired from the additional weight of the halo of thick clay that adds half an inch to my height. At some point I have either strayed from the road or the track has simply terminated under my feet, leaving me now stumbling across uneven and deep rutted fields, coarsely ploughed to allow the elements to do their worst. I would like to sit down but the land is wet and cold. Instead, I merely rotate where I stand, my line of sight tracking the passing headlights of some car still many miles across the fields. The land is flat like a billiard table; the only deviations are the deep, man-made irrigation channels and the occasional line of low hedgerow. In the summer there is a brilliant tapestry of mustard yellow and lilac, of rapeseed and linseed, but now little catches the eye. The fields are vast like oceans and, despite my weariness, I enjoy the sense of solitude and insignificance that the two empty hemispheres of black earth and sky allude to. But after a while such emptiness makes my thoughts morose and self-pitying, and I consider digging a grave. I wonder how deep I would have to dig to ensure that I would never be found. Deep enough so as not to be dug up by animals or eventually turned over by the endless tilling of the great farming machines.

Even as I consider them, I recognise my thoughts to be little more than theoretical. I have no intention of killing myself. Here, I have at least had the clarity to discriminate between finding little meaning in life and a desire or justification for ending it. If I had I would certainly not come here.

Also, if I had planned to kill myself, I doubt I would have brought so much food with me. My pockets are full of biscuits, most of which have now crumbled into a granular powder which gets under my fingernails as I shield my hands from the cold. I have also brought a rucksack, which cuts and chafes at my shoulders. This is a new addition to my nocturnal walks and I trawl through my fragmented memory to recall my intention. The bag suggests something more than a few hours silently patrolling deserted streets. My escape into the open countryside hinted that I may have finally put the vague plan of leaving home into action. I have run away from home on numerous occasions before, most of my efforts proving so ineffective and half-hearted that I was back home before anyone had even realised that I had left.

My conviction always wanes quickly. In one instance, a fundamental drive never to see my parents, the house or the town again crumbled before I even got to the end of my drive. On another occasion, I was simply overcome with a crushing fatigue, exhausting me only a few hundred yards from my front door. Ultimately, it is the futility of the enterprise which stops me. The distance I place between myself and my house, my school, or Dr Attwood's office is immaterial. The distance I place between myself and this world remains the same. It remains zero no matter which unit of measurement I use.

The contents of the backpack are typical of my disordered thinking. Much of the contents hint at some vague intention to walk far or not to return at all. I have packed warm clothes and food. Although I do not drink alcohol, I have brought a little bottle of brandy stolen from my father's cabinet, and objects loosely associated with such a venture: a knife, a watch and my toothbrush. Yet the sack is much heavier than necessary as I have retained three school textbooks and, apart from their value in enabling me to light a fire, these are completely useless. Whether I packed these items deliberately or whether they were just in the bag when I began packing, I could not tell you.

Despite the cold and the mud I like it here. When compared with my daily routine of home, school, and the carousel of hospitals, it seems like some sort of dislocated state, and the absence of people, noise, and clutter is liberating. *Do I wish to be alone?* It is a question I have asked myself a number of times. I cannot deny that the absence of violence would be welcome, but there is more to this than that. I certainly recoil from human company, my recurring fantasy is to wake one morning to find myself alone in the world. I understand that desiring this is not that unfamiliar. Yet, while others might use this event to explore their world, free from the constrictions of their society, free to steal, free to use the world's resources purely for their own whims, I do not think I would do any of these things. I have done all these things through my dislocations and the idea retains little appeal. Were I truly the last one left I don't think I would go very far at all. In the main, I think I'd probably stay in my room.

The open, empty countryside does, however, raise interesting questions and I find myself deliberating on whether people, even in their catatonic states during my dislocations, are still needed. Without them, as I am now, does my existence become even more meaningless, void of any point of reference and context? Were I to remain here in this field would my condition improve? Or might I find another dark corner, a deeper recess, and some unfathomable abyss, into which my malfunctioning state might fall? The thought excites and scares me in equal measure, cancelling out the conflicting emotions to leave a numbing, inconclusive, and undecided state. Then again, perhaps this is just the cold and the absence of stimulus in the bland monochrome landscape.

It is the biscuits that suddenly remind me of Dorothy, and in a moment's panic I look around, half-expecting to find her shuffling amongst the furrows. I hope I did not attempt to bring her with me: this would be far too far for her to walk and Mrs Parker would be most upset and angry. I am pretty sure I would not have brought her but I struggle to shake the lingering concern, imagining her poor old brittle body shaking in the cold, tied to a lamppost at the point at which my patience snapped and I pressed on without her. It is this more than anything else that turns me around and forces me to begin my weary trudge back across the ploughed field. Now that it is lighter I can see the road a hundred yards to my left. I guess if I owned a phone I could call my father to collect me. Though I am still far from sure where I am and I am not entirely sure he would come. I find myself hoping for the police car to come past. I suspect they might give me a lift, though this, too, is only likely to enrage my father. For the want of anything else to do, I am beginning to think a career in the police service may be my calling. There is something about the futility of their work, the endless unsocial hours and countless flawed and tragic encounters which seems to fit neatly with my personal experiences. However, I don't think I would like the uniform, or the attention.

XXIX

I am too cold to shiver, standing, as close as I dare, to the edge of the pond. It has not snowed, rather, the clear skies of the previous night have left a thick frost, which gives a satisfying crunch under my feet. Though this brilliant white sheen has not lasted long, taking only a few hours of watery sunshine to burn it back into small pockets that lurk under trees, leaving only its memory, and wet muddy footmarks. Similarly, the film of ice across the pond has also shrunk away. Earlier it too had been like a perfect plane of dark glass and now only translucent fragment can be seen, and these seem in some moribund struggle to hold their tips above the level of the water. There are no water birds, and only the occasional solitary bubble belches up from the depths. There is little wind, not enough to ripple the ink-like surface, but enough to slowly push the flotsam and jetsam, enabling it to accumulate to my right, amongst the great banks of unruly reeds.

It had been a very fine day, the low sun requiring sunglasses, reminding those wrapped in quilts and layers of the promise of summer. Now, the long fingers of the shadows have crossed the park, grown fat in their lattice, to create a uniform gloom. The once brilliant sun is spent and vague, a dirty smear of orange that requires hundreds of fluorescent streetlights to supplement its dying warmth.

I am no longer sure how long I have been standing here. The numerous dislocations potentially doubling, or even tripling, what may have been many hours. Despite this, for the majority, I estimate I have moved at best three feet from where I currently stand, catatonically staring into the pond, revolving though the cyclic seasons of negative emotions. I am, at least, pretty sure it has been over an hour since I stopped crying; my eyes feel tired, but the cold has thankfully stripped away the swelling, erasing the flushed pink, to return my complexion to its usual colourless pallor.

Now, across the park, I see a familiar shape approaching. My father walks slowly, dragging the vague shape of his fishing waders behind him. He looks grim and tired, probably still struggling with the disjointed explanation I gave him before my account degenerated into erratic and indecipherable screams.

"You alright, Francis?" asks my father. Despite only a short walk he is already out of breath, and this only gets worse as he struggles into his waders. "Just point, OK."

I raise my hand to direct him to a broad darkening mass of reeds, but this act alone is enough to start me crying again. Though, by now, it is too dark to distinguish the shape from the vegetation.

My father sets off in a clockwise march around the pond, pausing to find himself a long stick, before crashing clumsily into the rushes. His is a slow and laborious incursion, each and every step is a battle against the clotting roots and thick stinking mud, his head torch blinks as it scans back and forth amongst the foliage. Finally, as though emerging from some forest, the reeds by the edge of the water part, and he crashes out into the pond, his heavy form creating a small bow wave that ripples across the placid surface. For a briefest of seconds I catch a glimpse of the body, causing me to emit a pained and horrified screech, the pale fur serving as a stark contrast to the inky pool.

Though now twelve feet from the bank the water is still not that deep, having risen to only just below my father's groin. This too only serves to sharpen my self-rebuke, adding further guilt to my tortured incriminations. I find myself muttering apologies, while, from the pouch at the front of his waders, my father flaps a large plastic bag into the air, allowing the canopy to open. Now, with both hands deep in the bag, he delves down into the water, inverting the bag around the lifeless form, and raising it to his chest. The additional weight makes his movements even more cumbersome, and it is another minute and a half before he had successfully pivoted, to begin waddling in the direction of the bank.

172

"Thank you, Dad."

My father gives a sad smile, and gently lays the black bag on the ground to allow the excess water to drain away.

"Francis," implores my father, as I reach down to lift the plastic, "you don't have to look if you don't want to."

But I want to look, and I peel back the sheet to reveal the soaked, half frozen, body of Dorothy. Perhaps it is the cataracts in her eyes, but the empty stare does at least suggest she is peaceful. The cold water has stripped her body of warmth, leaving only a damp wet smell of pond weed, and none of her usual musty odour.

"What do you want to do with her, Francis?"

I offer no answer, extending my fingers to run them through the wet fur, unbuckling the little collar and dropping it into my pocket.

"We can bury her in the garden, if you like."

As much to prevent any more questions, I offer a slow nod, and my father gathers the ends of the bag in his hands before hauling the remains of Dorothy up to his chest. Without further comment, to the repetitive squelch of my father's rubber waders, we begin our sad procession back home.

"What happened, Francis?" asks my father. His voice is low and with emphasised tenderness, no doubt fearing another emotional eruption.

"I don't know, I guess she chased a bird onto the ice."

To this my father just nods grimly in response, presumably in recognition of the ridiculousness of the lie, but he does not challenge me. There was no ice, there were no birds, and even if they were, we both know that that arthritic creature could never have given chase, even if it had, by some miracle, seen them. I am now seized with dread as to what I am going to say to Mrs Parker.

"I'm sorry, Francis," says my father.

My mind casts back to that morning's walk, and our almost glacial shuffle around the small park, the majority of the distance achieved only through the continual gentle tug on the lead. The weekend walk in the park had become a regular feature of our little outings. My father drives us to the gates, as otherwise I doubt Dorothy could manage the distance.

The park is broadly circular, ringed with a dense perimeter of various foliage-stripped trees, the sympathetic landscaping hiding many of the ugly red-bricked houses that encroach around it. The pond is roughly near the centre, overlooked by an old statue of some Victorian identity. Now, despite whatever his past achievements may have been, he only collects bird droppings, and serves as some impromptu sundial, his lengthening shadow sweeping across the various concrete paths that criss-cross the grass.

As a rule, I tend not to go that close to the pond. This is not so much due to my aversion to water but because of the focus that that it represents, attracting the broad spectrum of park users, to feed the animals or enjoy their lunch. But today, despite the weather, it was deserted, and Dorothy had coaxed me in this direction, either having caught some scent, or simply wishing to take the shortest route home.

From this vantage point, I had stopped to take in the full array of humanity on offer that morning. My eyes were initially drawn to the joggers, their brightly coloured Lycra, periodically visible through the trees, as they continued their exhausting laps of the park. There were also other dog walkers, predominantly stationary, while their various animals raced frenetically after thrown objects, or tacked back and forth in the longer grass. Women pushed buggies and drank coffee out of paper cups, their children hidden under coats and hats, mummified from the cold. Old men sat on benches; in the summer they play chess, but that morning it was too cold to consider strategy, and heavily gloved hands would have knocked over the pieces. In the far corner, coloured tape had sealed off a particular tree like it was a crime scene, and the sound of chainsaws could be heard over the traffic. A father entertained some toddler with a ball, nimbly dodging the infant's clumsy efforts, the game only stopping after the child had fallen over, and had begun to cry. Others simply crossed the park, staying to the paths: shoppers, young couples, boys on bicycles, and Rebecca Shiels.

She approached confidently across the grass, her entourage in tow, a smug confidence clearly visible, savouring the prospect of some extra-curricular entertainment. I suspect she hoped I would run, to either enjoy the comical display of my pathetic flight, or to afford her pack some sport. Dorothy remained oblivious, sniffing and licking at some discarded sweet wrapper.

A cursory glance around the park offered little hope of assistance. It was as though each and every one of them had sought to offer this girl some degree of privacy, turning their backs or simply taking their leave of absence.

I had also underestimated her, having becoming too reliant on past experiences, expecting some precursory dialogue, some foreplay, to the humiliation or assault. But today she did not say a word, and she stepped briskly forward to deliver a slow underarm punch to my gut.

"You fucking rat on me again, Francis, and I, I…"

The barely contained rage had scrambled her thoughts, and she left the sentence unfinished. The accusation of being a rat was unfair, and this was selective memory on her part. I would challenge the assumption that I had in some way deliberately, and cynically, chosen to lose consciousness as part of some overarching strategy to see her suspended from school. The tardy arrival of Mr Beckley, having entered the class to discover Rebecca knelt over my prone figure, had not required my testimony to draw his own conclusions.

The punch was not even that hard, but my stomach reacted with unfamiliar sensitivity, twisting into knots. I kept my eyes on the ground, listening to the rapid breathing of my attacker, and the various taunts of her friends.

"Right!"

I heard Rebecca clearing her nostrils and felt the phlegm strike against my ear. But it was when she grabbed my wrist and began to drag me in the direction of the pond that the flash of panic surged through my body, realising her intention. She had pulled me only a yard towards the pond when I became consumed with mania, thrashing and wailing with my disordered fight for my survival. My memory of that instance is now only vague and disjointed, the singular desire to flee from the threat of the water having obliterated all other concerns.

Somehow, through a combination of my slaps and jerks, I had managed to pull my hand free, and it was only as I heard the squeaking yelp of Dorothy that I realised that I had relinquished the lead in the process. Yet, to my shame, I still continued my retreat on all fours, my nails digging into the wet earth, to place as much distance between myself and this threat as possible.

I turned to look back at the worst possible moment. I recall seeing Rebecca holding Dorothy by the scruff of her neck, the poor animal twisting to free itself from her careless grip. Then, with an almost dismissive swing of her arms, and a final curse, she hurled the animal in the direction of the water.

I had expected the animal to contort, to athletically adjust in mid-air, with the agility of a cat. But it was as though the old dog had become leaden. With only a faint whimpering howl, audible over my own visceral screams, she slapped heavily against the surface of the pond. By the time I could dislocate, the poor animal was submerged, and only the violent disruption of its impact could be seen.

Time resorted to the sound of mocking laughter. My cries now reduced to erratic sobs as my eyes filled with tears. Yet the fear of the inherent threat of the water still gripped me, and though I plead and prayed, Dorothy did not resurface.

"Fuck, Becca."

I recall it was Alison's voice, a sense of nervousness creeping into her tone, smothering the earlier moments of revelry.

"Dogs can swim, right?"

"Shit."

I had stopped screaming, a stunned disbelief had left me frozen. Something within me was still imploring me to take decisive action, but I could barely move a muscle. The cluster of girls had blocked my view of the pond, yet I expected at any moment to see Dorothy come tottering up the bank, shaking the icy water from its threadbare coat.

"Your dog is drowning, Francis," Rebecca said, turning back to me. It was a statement of fact, taunting and with a hint of pride. "In you go, Francis. Better make it quick, eh?"

I did not move; a pathetic plea bubbled up in my throat and frothed limply between my lips.

"Come on, Francis."

"Shit, Becca." It was Alison's voice again, agitated, and she bent down, pulling at her shoe laces.

"Leave it, Ally."

"Becca, I…"

"No! It is Francis's fucking dog. If she is going to be such a bitch about it, then it is her fucking problem."

The ripples of the water had died away, erasing the blemish, holding Dorothy somewhere within the darkness.

"Come on, Francis; it went in, at most, three feet from the bank."

"Shit."

Rebecca wrestled with her coat, and pulled out her phone. For one brief moment my naivety got the better of me, and I imagined her making some urgent call to the fire brigade or the school. But she only held the phone in front of her, slowly passing it back and forward, scanning the pool for sign of movement. Finally, she turned back around, pointing the phone in my direction.

"Care to say a few words for posterity, Francis?"

I blinked three times, before vomiting down my coat.

In my head, even long after the girl had lost interest and wandered away across the park, I had still imagined some dynamic rescue. It took many minutes to sufficiently conquer my fear, to begin to edge closer to the edge of the pond. Yet, with each step, I still conjured numerous scenarios in which I was somehow able to affect a rescue. In one, I imagined I reached out to grasp the lead, hauling Dorothy from the water. In others, I dislocated, stepping gingerly onto the water to lift the animal to safety. In each of these memories she is fine: shaken, and scared, but still something I can hold to myself and attempt to warm as I run back home.

It took over half an hour for these fantasies to fade, and in all this time I also clung to the hope she might have somehow swam, unnoticed, across the pond. I found myself scanning the park, calling her name in hope she might lift her head from within the long weeds that lined the bank. There was only a dull hollowness left by the time I spotted the small island of sodden grey fur that brushed the tensile membrane of the pond. Some hidden undercurrent had carried her away from the bank, retaining only sufficient buoyancy to stop her sinking without trace.

Numb, my thoughts circled in an endless loop, stumbling in search of some way I could feasibly explain this to Mrs Parker.

XXX

I sit crouched on the toilet of my preferred cubicle. I have been here now for over twenty minutes; long enough to determine that there are no new additions to the graffiti, no particular updates on Francis's activities. It is also long enough for me to get pins and needles in my feet. I like this sensation: it aches but is not unpleasant. I have never been poisoned but this is a mild version of what I imagine it to feel like: the crackling input from confused neurons, warning my brain of the unfolding concerns; the stress position starving muscles of oxygenated blood.

Dead arms are the same: the sensation you get when you awake with the limb trapped beneath you. It is like a rebellion has taken place. In the night, a coup d'état has occurred and the arm has declared independence from the tyranny of the brain. When you consider the maladministration of Francis's brain this is not wholly irrational. My lingering hope is that revolution might spread to the rest of my body, completing the work my arm has started, submerging me in my entirety to this strange, tingling existence. Sadly, though corrupted, Francis's brain is not that easily conquered; the blood returns and through the tingle of the sporadic fighting the insurrection is brutally crushed.

Someone has entered the bathroom; I hear the sound of heels approaching across the tiled floor. I listen to the systematic search of the bathroom, the methodical check of every stall, the heavy doors crashing back on their hinges. I do not even consider dislocating and I am surprised it has taken them so long to search for me here; it seems unfair to now cheat them of their victory. The search is conducted by Mrs Lawrence, my long-suffering history teacher. She does not seem surprised to see me but does look pained at my presence, her lip wobbling from a tense frustration. She is a tall woman, but has a certain old-fashioned style which gives a languid flow to her movements. In class she speaks eloquently, illustrating her words with graceful gestures of slender hands. But this composure seems to have deserted her and the barely constrained emotions give a jerking intensity to her movements. She fidgets impatiently while I gather my satchel and put my shoes on.

"School is closed, Francis. The headmistress has sent everyone home."

I seek no clarification and although I comply meekly I detect a croaking strain to her voice, an unstable anger, and when I look at her she is curiously reluctant to hold my gaze. Her face looks gaunt and there is a red tint to her eyes. I think she may have been crying.

"Leave by the Weston Road gate, Francis. Francis? Did you hear me? The Weston Road gate."

Though it is still mid-morning I pass no one as I move through the building, and the school yard is equally empty. Only when I get to the school gate do I find two more members of the teaching staff. I can't recall their names but they look tired and haunted; they watch me approach and pass without comment, pulling the gate closed behind me.

Despite my numerous truancies I am now at a loss as to what to do with myself. The ejection from the school premises is unexpected, and for a moment I wonder whether my confusion has once again got the better of me. Is it the half term holidays? I think not. I distinctly remember those other children in uniform this morning and as I turn the corner into Weston Road I notice a small cluster of figures dressed in the green blazers of my school's uniform. These are girls I recognise, one being my nemesis in fact, but something about the body language is wrong. They stand in a huddle, arms around each other in some clumsy embrace. Orbiting them like satellites are three boys from my year. I recognise them as well but don't recall their names. They look confused and angry, pacing with their own thoughts. Something has happened in school.

Weston Road is long and were they to look up they would see me. I would like to dislocate, to slip past them, but even for my now well trained abilities this distance would be beyond my lung capacity. So I approach with fingers crossed, hopeful that whatever it is that has shut the school is sufficiently important to render me unimportant. Yet as I pass them my curiosity gets the better of me. There is something about the scene that stirs my failing memories and my brain begins trawling for clues.

The boys eye me with contempt but hold their own counsel. Eventually, my lingering presence is detected and the girls turn to face me. Two of the girls have been crying, Rebecca Shiels one of them, while the moronic Alison Townsend tries to comfort her. Their makeup is smeared down swollen eyes and they look diseased, as though suffering some monumental allergic reaction. The beeps from the phones in their pockets go unanswered. At first they stare at me stupidly, their mouths open, as though they are not entirely sure what they are looking at. But after a pronounced delay their confusion finally morphs into anger; their faces harden and contort with venomous cruelty.

"Go fuck yourself, Kelly. You are such a fucking Freak."

I blink three times but offer no riposte. These are words I have heard many times before, often chanted so as to draw support from bystanders. Today, though, there is something missing, a lack of confidence or conviction in their statement. Despite this, the abuse is sufficient to satisfy my curiosity and I give a little smile before turning to walk away. Yet today my usually reliable attackers do not follow me, choosing instead to only hurl further verbal abuse and a solitary rock which rattles past me, having missed by a distance. I had not walked far and it was a poor, ill-directed throw. Standards of victimisation seem to be slipping, as does the attitude to my continual school absences. It is as though my indifference to myself is becoming infectious. Something in me considers picking it up like some faithful dog and bringing it back. "You've dropped this," I imagine myself saying. Thankfully, the thought is fleeting and looking over my shoulder I notice the group has now closed ranks and is slowly wandering away in the opposite direction.

It has come back to me now. I had arrived late for school but had I intended to go to class I would have probably not missed much more than ten minutes of the lesson. Not that it mattered, for at the school gate it was as though half the school were waiting for me in the playground. Not that they *were* waiting for me. The vast majority, students and teachers alike, were not even aware of my arrival; their backs remained turned, craning their necks; their gaze rarely shifted from the upper floors of the great concrete monstrosity which represents the sizable core of this educational facility. They chattered excitedly amongst themselves, only momentarily turning to a friend as if to verify their disbelief of what they were witnessing.

The building is four storeys in height: the uninspiring slabs of concrete tainted by the stains of rusted guttering and running water. It is a tired construction and cracked window frames house only thin expanses of single-glazed glass: a factor that requires the heating systems to fight constantly to raise the temperature of the classrooms by even fractions of a degree in the colder months. Though the warmer months remain little more than distant memories I noticed a large number of the windows were open. Teachers stood at each like sentries, and others could be seen scuttling back and forth between classrooms.

In the absence of anything to do, I joined the back of this assembled mob. More teachers mingled amongst the crowd, making half-hearted efforts to corral the crowds into lessons. But mostly these also watched with horror and helplessness at the unfolding acrobatics, as the small nimble figure continued to shimmy up the black metal guttering.

The occasional shout of encouragement was browbeaten and supressed by the teachers. Meanwhile, the spider-like figure of Billy Rowley seemed to be taking a rest barely a few feet from the roof of the building. He was at best three feet from the nearest open window and I recognised Monsieur Grimshaw's beckoning hands, coaxing him towards the safety of the classroom. If this was part of the headmistress's strategy, considering what happened in detention, this was a poor choice of negotiator. Two other teachers waited above the boy, taking it in turns to peer nervously over the edge at their prize, still frustratingly out of reach.

Even when the headmistress pushed her way into the centre of the crowd, the gathering spectators refused to move. She barked orders but her voice remained strangely suppressed as though she might startle the boy from his perch. Rebecca yelled "Jump!" and Alison laughed.

Another yelp of appreciation rose from the crowd and this time Billy heard it, turning his head to look down to the many faces below. At that moment it was as though he was looking directing at me and though from this distance his eyes were just little black pits. I sensed our gaze meet, but could derive no understanding of his mind or intentions. It was just as a grin began to form in the corners of my face that it happened. Though I now remember what happened, I remain hazy about certain details. It was as though part of me felt a premonition, as though watching the scene as a repeat of an earlier episode. I am, however, convinced that I heard the sound, a pronounced popping noise, just a fraction of a moment before there was a collective intake of breath from those assembled, anticipating the panic. To my left a girl clamped her hand over her mouth and with primitive reflexes everybody froze as though dislocated. It was at this point that I remembered my experiment with the eggs.

The scream was ignited by a loud clatter as the length of guttering, a heavy fixture of cast metal, toppled from the wall to ring out like some malformed bell against the weather-eaten concrete of the school yard. Most were now silent, so quiet that the groan of the bending guttering was clearly heard as Billy's weight prised it from the side of the building.

There were more sounds of metal striking concrete: this time the rain-like rattle of screws, prised from the wall, bouncing away to be lost in the nearby lawn.

My first instinctive dislocation was premature and it was still far from certain what was to unfold. Billy was still high in the air, still in contact with the side of the building, but his posture was all wrong, his legs hung in free space and his back arched. From this angle, we could only see the back of his head - but the frozen expression of the teacher on the roof above him mirrored the horrified moment of realisation, telling us all we needed to know. I breathed out and quickly sucked in a fresh lungful to arrest time once more. By then, the unfolding disaster was certain. Billy hung in mid-air, a single arm still groping for the broken guttering above him.

Around me the stagnant audience provided a snapshot of the unfolding realisation. Some stared blankly, just the slight dilation of pupils suggesting the adrenalin response to the impending danger. Others had begun to cringe as though expecting to be struck, already turning away, protecting themselves from the final moments of gravity's victory.

Picking a path through the crowd took more effort than I anticipated and I was forced to steal another breath before I was able to tack my way through the massed ranks. I was, however, now confident that my interventions would remain unseen. Only the teachers seemed unable to tear away their gaze, the ensemble of students having already shielded their eyes from the terrible impact. The teachers would not see me, they continued to look up and I was just one small, uniform-clad figure. Eye witness accounts in such instances are always so unreliable.

Billy was now only two floors above the ground. In his fall he had contorted, cat-like, but I was under no illusion as to his ability to land with similar poise or dexterity. The teacher on the roof was also gone, part due to the narrowing perspective as I approached and part from the understandable desire to not witness the inevitable. Yet, at the window, Monsieur

Grimshaw seemed to have denied himself such a luxury. His expression was that of pure frozen pain; his arms still stretched far out in front of him, his round, soft body so far from the window ledge that there was a genuine risk that he might topple after his pupil.

My next breath was even shorter. Too short, in fact, as Billy was still too high for me to reach and I had done little to replenish my air supply. Though it was this quiet moment of reflection that enabled me to consider what I was doing. For at that moment I was back in detention vomiting over my desk. I was back at home, fleeing from the safety of my room. At that moment I was walking Dorothy, standing in the cold, squinting through the blackened tendrils of shadow-like branches for some strange bird. Finally, at the moment my lungs began to convulse, I was recoiling in horror as that soft overbearing face pressed itself to my own. And now I was here: exposed, dislocated in front of an audience of over one hundred members of my distrusted peers.

I turned to look at the static figures. All had now turned, raising their arms across their faces, and would not witness my intervention. But that was not the point. The point was Billy Rowley. It was this boy who gate-crashed into those small spaces, denying me those few crumbs of comfort that prevent me from shattering into a thousand pieces; those few private places that I can call my own.

Billy had turned to face the ground which, in his own mind, would now be rushing up to meet him. Yet he seemed calm, his eyes open and his hands barely out in front of him to brace his fall. The plastic pill bottle had fallen from his top pocket; the lid had been lost and I could see a number of his tablets sharing his descent.

Here, Dr Attwood, here is the true object of my discomfort. This boy, hung above me. This is the thing that threatens to totally obliterate whatever limited existence you think you have found in me. I guess you cling to it in the hope that it will grow, out of some deluded but well-intended hope that it might help. This boy clings to it; my parents, Monsieur

186

Grimshaw, and Mrs Parker all cling to it. And each of you seek to pull me in conflicting directions. I cannot even begin to comprehend by what strange twist of fortune I have not already been torn into shreds.

I stepped back three paces and exhaled. The impact was like a wet thud and I was close enough to hear the faint percussion of the erupting mist of Billy's blood raining onto the school yard. The collective wail of anguish turned to erratic screams and running feet as the mob fled in confusion. But I did not turn to witness the ensuing mayhem. My eye-line was drawn to Monsieur Grimshaw: his body bent double over the window frame, his face buried in his hair-covered hands. Above him, high over the top of the building, a sliver of blue pierced the blanket of ever-shifting grey sky. It seemed so long since the start of winter it was almost as though I had forgotten what the sky looked like. It was only a moment before the clouds reformed, smothering what limited promise it had evoked. But this was enough, like some part of my brain had awoken from a deep and dreamless hibernation.

The following day, news of Billy Rowley's death makes the local newspaper. The article is long with many letters for me to colour in and it takes most of the morning to make sure I have done a diligent job. But it is time well spent as it is during this process that, somewhere close to the bottom of the first column, I have what I can only describe as an epiphany. The process of colouring in letters is continually hampered by the continuous need to change pens. The endless lifting and dropping is a strain to my wrist and I have a tendency to lose pen lids in the process. This dries out my pens, shortening their life span considerably. By taping them together I now can work much more efficiently. My first effort resulted in the tips being too close together, causing annoying little coloured marks across the otherwise immaculate page, which ruins the effect. I then tried taping them facing in opposite directions, which solved this particular problem but resulted in me needing to change grip after each coloured letter and totally defeated the point of taping them together in the first place. Now, with the aid of a small wedge of paper, the tips are sufficiently far apart, at an angle, and it now takes only a subtle manipulation of my fingers to change grip and continue colouring. This constitutes a significant improvement.

My mother is more morose than usual, and I have not seen my father all day.

XXXI

The weather is much better and my classmates no longer huddle like chickens at the bus stop. Yet these loose groups only give the illusion of conversation. Most, even those surrounded by close friends, remain hunched over their phones, mostly only looking up to distract their neighbour to show them what they are watching or have just typed. Such moments are greeted with shrill laughs or sniggers. Their inane chatter is punctuated by bleeps and ring tones. The girls just giggle and preen but the boys, at least, are a little more animated. Proper fights are rare but they are continually seeking to commit some act of comedic violence against each other. Usually, this is just the endless cycle of practical jokes and puppyish pushing and shoving. My attention is currently being held by two boys battering each other with flailing gym kits: the blows unbalance them but they are otherwise harmless, the timing of the swings seemingly coordinated so that they take it in turn to hit each other.

There are three hard plastic seats under the canopy of the bus stop, but with the absence of Mrs Parker and Derrek I have all of them to myself. My classmates recoil from my proximity, preferring to enjoy the first signs of spring: a windless, clear-skied day that hints at the promise of summer. The lipstick scrawl is now so smudged that I can't read what Francis Kelly has been up to. But someone else has been diligent, carving letters into the blistered paintwork of the frame with either a knife or some keys.

"BR - RIP."

It takes me time to work out the significance of these five hyphenated letters, the memory of the incident having faded quickly in my thoughts. The immediate novelty and shock to my classmates was soon choked by the swift return of routine. The familiar cycle of institutional life and the insignificant jealousies and concerns of teenagers have regained the initiative, creeping over the collective consciousness like an overcast day. The insincerity of the outpouring of grief has now been demonstrated by its transience. I include myself in this analysis. It did not take long for the lengthening shadow to obscure the memory of this boy, the recollection of our history degrading to the point that this hastily scrawled act of vandalism is all that is tangibly left. He has become 'that boy that fell from the roof', a testament to the realisation that nobody could truly claim to have known him at all. He is now a blank canvas, an identity to which even the most fanciful of rumours and innuendo can be attributed. Distasteful jokes have also begun to circulate.

Finally, the lumbering hulk of the school bus rolls into view, shudders to a stop and announces its arrival with the hydraulic hiss of brakes. My classmates sullenly begin to converge at the doors; even now their eyes rarely raise from their phones, navigating by the vague awareness of the shuffling child in front of them. There is only an approximation of a queue, as these uniformed figures are pressed through the doors, taking their allotted seats in the intricate social hierarchy of the bus. I watch through the windows as they collapse wearily into various chairs or stow bags above their heads. The two boys battling with their gym bags now continuing to air their grievances by repeatedly punching each other on the bicep and shoulder, toppling onto other friends who push back to reclaim their space. Those inmates already inside peer down in search of friends, waving or making obscene hand gestures which are quickly reciprocated. Some catch my eye, and they stare accusingly.

Though the last passenger has stepped on board the bus belligerently refuses to leave. It sits with the doors open, the engine idly ticking over while my classmates become increasingly impatient, many turning their attention to the window to study the singular cause of the delay. I feared this would happen. In the winter months this is less of a problem: the doors are quickly swung closed to keep out the cold and the darkness of those gloomy mornings camouflages me from the driver's mirror. But now it waits, challenging my obstinacy. I have long suspected that my repeated absence would ultimately lead to such a recalcitrant standoff. This now becomes a test of nerve, or, more accurately, a battle between my unwillingness to submit to my education and the less understood forces of the bus driver's impatience and the pressures of his timetable.

There is a short, impatient blast of the bus's horn and I dig my hands into my pockets as though to demonstrate my continual resistance; after a few more seconds the driver blinks first and concedes defeat. It is the growing clamour of my classmates behind him that has come to my aid, fostering the understandable desire in the driver to be free of the gaggle of whooping apes in uniform. I pity the bus driver; his is not a job I would willingly perform. If I was required to do so I am pretty sure I would drive these children far out into the countryside and make them walk from a different isolated location each morning.

There is a bitter hiss as the doors close, and as the bus pulls into the traffic I watch to ensure it does actually leave. Above the sound of the engine I hear a rumble of small fists. The panes of the windows vibrate as a few of my classmates pummel the glass with their palms. I cannot tell whether this is as a salute to my defiance or to mock me for the consequences of my self-imposed isolation. I momentarily dislocate to savour my victory. When I breathe out I find myself at the epicentre of a peaceful scene.

"You've missed the bus again."

Mrs Parker stares blankly across the street from the seat beside me, her mouth hanging open, poised to say more. I guess she is watching the few dirty pigeons that now bob and strut around the overfilling waste bin, flicking at cigarette ends before waddling off in disgust. Her observation requires no comment but I nod to acknowledge the accuracy.

It has been a while since I have seen Mrs Parker. She is still dressed in the same night shirt and dressing gown and, though it has not rained for a couple of days, I do not imagine that her tartan slippers are the most durable of footwear. In the daylight her skin now seems like creased wax paper and, while she wears no makeup, her mist-coloured hair remains neatly fastened into pink and sky blue rollers.

I apologise for not going to her funeral but, I tell her, I did not know when it was. I admit that I have not recently been to see Derrek either, but Mrs Parker does not seem concerned. It is only now, pausing to perfect my delivery, that I tell Mrs Parker that we have had to put down Dorothy, nervously studying her dead features for the impact of my well-meaning lie. Whether she believes me or not I cannot tell, but, regardless, she does not seem particularly upset.

Now, the bridgehead secured, the lies come more easily and I tell her that, in the end, it was her back legs that gave up. I claim that the vet's diagnosis was that her kidneys had stopped working. I mention I had suspicions that my father was pleased with this outcome but Mrs Parker concedes that had it not been that, it would have been something else. She tells me that she had a habit of giving Dorothy chocolate, not knowing that this is very bad for dogs. By the time she found out Dorothy was already old and she did not see the point in depriving her of a little treat now and again.

"It was the same with Derrek," she says, "he used to like to smoke and, while I had never liked the habit, I would have let him continue had he not nearly burnt the house down."

The children have left a great deal of sweet wrappers, and though she does not mention it I think this annoys Mrs Parker. As a consolatory gesture I spend a few minutes picking a few of them up, and put them in my pocket. But otherwise we spend the time in silence, the noise of the traffic the only backdrop to our private thoughts. I imagine things are a bit easier for Mrs Parker now she does not have to look after Derrek. I tell Mrs Parker that we buried Dorothy in the garden and I ask her whether she has seen her dog, but Mrs Parker changes the subject.

"So what you going to do, Francis?"

I tell Mrs Parker that I don't know. I guess I will eventually bow to the inevitable and walk to school. I think my first class is geography, and my grades are pretty good so I should not get into too much trouble. It will most likely be either Mr Hardacre or Mrs Terrance who takes the detention. Neither trouble me unduly and I have brought my felt tip pens and a fresh newspaper to colour in.

"No," she says, "I mean what are you going to do about the other thing?"

I turn, as much out of surprise for her bringing up the issue as the implication of her question, but Mrs Parker does not flinch. She has a fantastic poker face. She offers no opinion, yet, by knowing she is aware of my deliberations, this somehow helps put my thoughts into context. As to this matter, I have yet to reach a firm conclusion and, though I tell Mrs Parker that things are a bit complicated, I realise that this is not a satisfactory answer. Mrs Parker's silence remains non-judgemental but I do detect a degree of disappointment. I feel she is trying to help me and I would not wish my reluctance to be misconstrued as ungratefulness.

"It's your decision, Francis. But the worst thing you can do is to waste time. Even if time is yours to control, even if you can dislocate."

I find myself nodding again. I like Mrs Parker and it is reassuring to know someone with whom you are able to share such things.

XXXII

I sit in the darkness, basking in the cold glow of the laptop on my knees, the only other light being the narrow slit of light at the bottom of my bedroom door. I only become aware of it in the very moment that it is extinguished and footsteps are heard on the landing, the prelude before my parents retire to bed. There is a light knock on the door.

"Don't stay up too late, Francis."

I do not answer, my attention remaining firmly on the screen of the computer. I am streaming a short video clip, less than twenty seconds long, yet I estimate I have now watched it over fifty times, stopping only occasionally to read the long list of glib comments underneath.

The footage is grainy and shaking; the initial footage just blurs as fingers fall in front of the lens, and muffled voices can be heard, but without comprehension. Then, in a broad sweep, the camera is turned to face a single protagonist. A small figure is kneeling on a wide lawn, her scrawny frame hidden amongst numerous layers of clothing. She is looking past the camera: an empty vacant stare, her features frozen in a grotesque mix of horror and denial.

"Care to say a few words for posterity, Francis?"

There is a noticeable pause before the solitary figure convulses, coughing a mucus drool of vibrant yellow liquid down herself.

The camera wobbles and I hear the sound of sniggering, the hilarity becoming too great for the camera to be kept steady. By the time the footage comes to an abrupt halt, it is facing down into the grass.

I have watched this repeatedly and with a cool detachment, an emotionless indifference, that is impressive, even for me. At that moment I feel no empathy, unable to connect the question posed with the violent response of that wretched figure.

I move the mouse a few millimetres, and click on replay.

XXXIII

"I received a call from your school," said Dr Attwood. "Your teacher told me about the accident in your class."

Dr Attwood's emphasis on the word 'accident' momentarily unnerves me, though for all concerned this was soon established as the only plausible explanation for what had happened.

"If you like," she continues, "we can talk about this."

For a brief moment, as we hold each other's gaze, I genuinely consider telling her everything. I could give Dr Attwood a detailed account of the method but, even to me, my motivation was less concrete. I could tell the doctor how I had kept a pair of surgical gloves from the previous science lesson and how I had worked them onto my hands beneath my desk while waiting for the suitable opportunity. Yet if I was to offer a full disclosure, I would also have to tell Dr Attwood that, as I arrived late for school that morning, there was no conscious thought about how I was to spend the day. I do not think it was even opportunism. Rather, like with the poor forearm of Dr Bennett, it was as though every single moment of both our lives, the infinitely small vibration of every atom in the universe, had been building to that particular moment. I could tell Dr Attwood that I am not sure I believe in the concept of free will, not in the theological sense at least.

The day was very much as anticipated by all concerned: the various shuffling of close-knit groups and clusters, trudging through rooms to be subjected to the cyclic rendition of academia. Finally, I found myself sitting in Mr Mason's English class. The classroom is an uninspiring place for anything inspiring. The walls are painted in what I can best describe as a cerebral grey; a fitting backdrop for the waffling drone of Mr Mason's voice, punctuated only briefly by the theatrical excess of the occasion. He has a habit of conducting the

196

majority of his lessons with his back to us, speaking as much to the text-covered wall as to his students. Having not turned for sustained periods, most of his class tend to look away from their diligent study to stare absentmindedly out of the window.

At the beginning of the lesson my own emotions bordered on the inert, the slowly gathering realisation having yet to foster any aspect of exhilaration or fear. Yet I recall the precise moment with crystal clarity. There was the nerve-shredding screech of a chair being moved, corresponding with some half-heard phrase of my teacher. I remain convinced that the words were not his, and it was the mellow voice of Mrs Parker that I heard.

Only now am I conscious of my silently predatory reconnaissance. It was as though I was now remembering the day from a different perspective, recalling how I had missed my opportunity in assembly and, despite searching throughout the lunch break and between lessons, my quarry could not be found. I had strolled the grounds at break and lunch with a strange confidence, though even then I was still not sure of my true intention.

Though I remain convinced I was of no firm decision as to my plan, I think my classmates knew, or at least suspected. For once I passed through crowds without reception, as though the latent threat oozed from me, emitting a certain toxicity which warned away some would-be assailant and ignited a primitive fear. That was, until Mr Mason's English class.

I had dislocated twice before finally, on the third attempt, I rose from my chair with clarity of purpose. Mr Mason's back was still turned and a thrown protractor would shortly reach the apex of its arched path across the classroom. On the whole, my fellow students remained hunched like convicts with only a few of the blank stares deviating from their books. Shuffling crablike down the narrow aisle of desks, I pivoted to face Rebecca. Her face was grotesque and stupid, her eyebrows raised, her tongue pushed firmly into her makeup-clad cheek, while behind me her odious friend mirrored her clownish features. Along with the books and papers on her desk, the array of stationary provided a more than adequate choice for my purposes. I selected a long, sharpened pencil, lifting and rotating it in space until the graphite point rested perpendicular to her mocking glare. The adrenaline had already depleted my oxygen reserves but my rage had sharpened my focus and I began to push the tip of the pencil towards the unflinching eyeball.

Despite all my preparations, and my elaborate fantasies of hurting this girl, this was the first time I had actually attempted to penetrate anything other than air or liquid while dislocated. This was an obvious oversight on my part. The effort required surprised me and I was forced to lean, my right hand pressed against the left, balled into a fist around the pencil, to generate sufficient force. Slowly, the whole body of my victim slid backwards in her chair; rather than allowing the pencil tip to puncture her cornea, once pressed against the back rest the chair itself begins to slide steadily into the desk behind. Changing strategy, I held the pencil in my right hand, gripping her wire-tight ponytail with the left as I pushed. Finally, the shaft began its slow insertion into the girl's eyeball. Millimetre by millimetre the pencil moved forward in a smooth soundless motion.

I estimate that about an inch of wood had been inserted into the girl's face before I was forced to abort my labours. My chest convulsed as I urgently shimmied with stuttering sideways steps back to my desk. Finally, collapsing into my chair, I made no effort to compose myself before my diaphragm crumbled and the stale air exploded from my lungs in staccato sobs. My first gasp for air was thankfully concealed by the violent scream of the girl clawing at her face, convulsing fitfully, failing to stem the explosion of blood and intraocular fluid into the face of Alison Townsend and across the shoulders of one of my classmates.

"Francis, do you think these sessions are helping?"

My answer is deliberately vague and offers little encouragement, delivered with a passive and obtuse indifference which I no longer care whether Dr Attwood will associate with introversion or bitterness. In the following silence, I look around the room and try and estimate the amount of time I have spent in this chair, mentally adding up the sessions.

Droplets of water from this morning's shower still cling to the glass on the open window; with time they will evaporate to leave nothing but the slightest of smears. The plants in Dr Attwood's office steadily rotate towards the window; a dying leaf withers. Dust gathers against all surfaces and with every scrawled word, ink depletes from the doctor's pen. Through this endless sequence of moments all that is organic decays and that which is metallic corrodes and rusts. The leather-bound books become brittle and flake, the carpets become threadbare; fibres are ground under feet and blown away on draughts or inhaled into vacuum cleaners. High above us clouds slowly roll to the east, their passage measureable to the naked eye only in reference to the scaffolding of a crane standing against the skyline. Invisible to human senses the planet rotates, radio waves radiate into space, thermals of heat circulate the air, cells replenish, the microscopic multiply and atoms vibrate about their mean positions. All things, by our own definitions, become older. I wonder whether I continue to age when dislocated or whether this is yet another benefit of non-existence.

Dr Attwood sits quietly and hopes for a more substantial answer, but all I give her is a watery but well-meaning smile. I shift my weight and allow myself to sink backwards into the soft embracing comfort of the richly upholstered chair.

THE END

Acknowledgements

I would like to thank Jonathan Curzon, Dr Carly Holmes and Lorena Goldsmith, at Daniel Goldsmith – Literary Consultants for their support and expertise to bring this book to completion. I would also like to thank Beach at Beach Studio for developing the cover artwork.

Please follow me on Twitter: @borealisnovel

Printed in Great Britain
by Amazon